Jumping to Conclusions

RACHEL YODER—
Always Trouble Somewhere

Book 7

Jumping to Conclusions

RACHEL YODER—
Always Trouble Somewhere

Book 7

BARBOUR
PUBLISHING

Published by Barbour Publishing, Inc., P.O. Box 719, Uhrichsville, Ohio 44683, www.barbourbooks.com

Our mission is to publish and distribute inspirational products offering exceptional value and biblical encouragement to the masses.

Member of the
Evangelical Christian
Publishers Association

Printed in the United States of America.

Dickinson Press Inc., Grand Rapids, MI; Print Code D10002201; February 2010

Dedication

To the students and teachers of the Walnut
Valley School near Walnut Creek, Ohio.
It was great getting to meet you!

Glossary

abastz—stop

ach—oh

an lauerer—eavesdropper

appeditlich—delicious

baremlich—terrible

bensel—silly child

blos—bubble

boppli—baby

bopplin—babies

brieder—brothers

bruder—brother

buwe—boy

bussli—kitten

daed—dad

danki—thanks

dumm—dumb

gaul—horse

grank—sick

grossdaadi—grandfather

grossmudder—grandmother

gut—good

heiraat—marriage

hund—dog

iem—bee

jah—yes

kapp—cap

katze—cats

kinner—children

kinskinner—grandchildren

kumme—come
lecherich—ridiculous
maedel—girl
mamm—mom
missverschtand—misunderstanding
munn—moon
naerfich—nervous
naas—nose
pescht—pest
peschte—pests
retschbeddi—tattletale
schmaert—smart
schnarixer—snorer
schnuppich—snoopy
schtann—stars
schteche—sting
schweschder—sister
umgerennt—upset
verhuddelt—mixed-up
wasser—water
windel—diaper
wunderbaar—wonderful
zoll—inches

Bass uff, as du net fallscht!	Take care you don't fall!
Guder mariye.	Good morning.
Ich kann sell net geh!	I cannot tolerate that!
Mir hen die zeit verbappelt.	We talked away the time.
Raus mitt!	Out with it!
She dich, eich, wider!	See you later!
Was in der welt?	What in all the world?
Wie geht's?	How are you?

Contents

Chapter 1

Good News

"I'm going out to get the mail!" Rachel Yoder called to her mother as she raced out the back door.

"Oh no, you don't!" Rachel's brother Jacob shouted as he dashed out the door behind her. "Getting the mail is Buddy's job!"

Rachel screeched to a halt and whirled around to face Jacob. "Since when is it Buddy's job to get the mail?"

"Since I started training him to open the mailbox." Jacob grinned at Rachel, and the skin around his blue eyes crinkled. "Today I'm gonna teach him how to take the mail from the box and then bring it to the house and put it on the kitchen table."

Rachel snickered and waved her hand. "Like that'll ever happen. That big, hairy *hund* [dog] of yours isn't *schmaert* [smart] enough to get the mail."

"*Jah* [Yes], he is. Buddy's the smartest dog I've ever owned," Jacob insisted.

"That's because he's the *only* dog you've ever owned." Rachel blinked her eyes several times. "Buddy's nothing but trouble!"

"Is not."

"Is too."

"Is not." Jacob pointed at Rachel. "You're the one who's trouble!"

Rachel frowned and shook her head. "I am not trouble!"

"Jah, you are."

"Am not."

"Are so."

"Am not. Buddy's the troublemaker, and he's not schmaert enough to get the mail!"

"He is so schmaert enough, and I'm gonna prove it to you right now!" Jacob dashed across the yard and yanked open the door to Buddy's dog run.

Woof! Woof! Buddy leaped off the roof of his doghouse, where he liked to sleep, and dashed out of the dog run. Then he raced to Rachel, put both paws on her chest, and—*slurp!*—licked her face.

"Yuck!" Rachel pushed Buddy down and swiped her hand across her face. "Stay away from me, you big, hairy beast! I don't want any of your slimy kisses!" She wrinkled her nose. "Besides, you have bad breath!"

Jacob chuckled and slapped his knee. "He's just letting you know how much he likes you. You should realize that by now."

"Humph!" Rachel folded her arms and glared at Jacob. "The only thing I realize is that Buddy's a big *pescht* [pest], and I don't enjoy his sloppy, stinky kisses!"

Jacob thumped Rachel's back. "You'll get used to them some day!" He clapped his hands and gave an ear-piercing whistle. "Come on, Buddy. Let's go get the mail!"

Buddy tore off down the driveway, barking all the way, and sending gravel flying in several directions.

Jacob sprinted behind the dog, yelling, "Go, Buddy! Go!"

Rachel followed. She was curious about how Buddy could get the mail.

When they reached the mailbox by the side of the road, Jacob grabbed the handle and yanked it open with a thunk! He waited a few seconds; then he closed it again. He did this several times. After the fifth time, he pointed to the mailbox handle and said, "Open it, Buddy. Open the mailbox!"

Woof! Woof! Buddy wagged his tail and stared at the mailbox as if to say, *What are you talking about?*

Jacob opened and closed the mailbox door several more times; then he said, "Open it, Buddy! Open the mailbox now!"

Much to Rachel's surprise, Buddy grabbed the handle on the mailbox in his teeth, pulled, and— *thunk!*—the door popped open.

Woof! Woof! Buddy wagged his tail and stared at the mailbox as if to say, *Look what I did!*

Rachel rushed forward to grab the stack of letters. Jacob stepped in front of her. "How's Buddy gonna learn to get the mail if you do it for him?"

Rachel rolled her eyes. "Buddy might be schmaert enough to open the mailbox, but he's not schmaert enough to take the mail out."

"Sure he is. Just stand back and watch."

"Whatever." Rachel stepped aside, even though she was sure Buddy would not take the mail out of the box.

Jacob pointed to the mail inside the box. "Get it, Buddy! Get the mail out of the box!"

Buddy tilted his head and whined.

Rachel shook her head. "He doesn't have a clue what you're talking about."

"Okay, then, I'll try it another way." Jacob reached into the mailbox, picked up one of the letters, opened Buddy's mouth, and put the letter between the dog's teeth. "You're a good hund!" He patted Buddy's head.

Buddy whimpered and nuzzled Jacob's hand with his big nose.

Rachel reached into the mailbox and snatched the rest of the mail. "I knew he wasn't schmaert enough to get the mail by himself."

"Hey!" Jacob frowned. "How am I supposed to train Buddy to get the mail if you take it first?"

"I don't care if Buddy learns how to get the mail. I just want to take the mail to the house, and—" Rachel stared at the letter in her hand. It was addressed to her. It was from her cousin Mary!

Mary was not only her cousin but had also been her best friend. Rachel had been very sad when Mary's family moved to Indiana.

"Yippee! I've got a letter from Mary! I've got a letter from Mary!" Rachel shrieked as she waved the letter in the air. "I'm going to the house to read Mary's letter. You and your schmaert dog can bring the rest of the mail whenever you're ready."

Rachel started to turn around, but Buddy dropped the letter in his mouth, leaped into the air, and snatched Mary's letter out of her hand!

"Give that back, you big, hairy mutt!" Rachel lunged for the letter.

Woof! Woof! Buddy took off on a run.

Rachel raced after him.

The dog zipped up the driveway, then turned and zipped back again. Rachel ran behind him, waving her hands and shouting, "*Abastz* [Stop]! You're a bad dog!"

Jacob doubled over with laughter as Rachel chased the dog. She'd just started down the driveway again when she spotted their friend Orlie Troyer walking up the driveway.

"Catch that *dumm* [dumb] hund!" she shouted to

Orlie. "Don't let him get away!"

Orlie cupped his hands around his mouth. "What?" he called.

"I said—"

Woomph! Buddy plowed into Orlie, knocking him to the ground. The letter flew out of Buddy's mouth.

Yip! Yip! Buddy tore across the field on the side of their property, yapping all the way.

"Bad dog!" Rachel shouted.

Jacob dashed after Buddy, waving his hands. "Come back here, Buddy! Come back here right now!"

Rachel ran down the driveway and dropped to her knees beside Orlie. "Are you all right? Buddy didn't hurt you, I hope."

Orlie shook his head. "Just knocked the wind out of me, that's all." He clambered to his feet and brushed the dirt from his trousers. "I think Buddy was excited to see me."

"Maybe so, but I think the real reason Buddy plowed into you was because he stole a letter from me and was trying to get away." Rachel snatched the letter Buddy had dropped. "It's from my cousin Mary in Indiana."

"How'd the hund get your letter?" Orlie asked.

Rachel groaned. "Jacob was trying to teach Buddy to get the mail."

"Guess he needs to teach him to come when he's called." Orlie chuckled as he pointed across the field. "Jacob's going to be tired by the time he catches Buddy."

"You mean *if* he catches the hairy hund." Rachel lifted Mary's letter. "I'm going to the house to read my mail. Do you want to come along?"

Orlie grinned. "Jah, sure. I'd like to hear what Mary has to say, too."

Rachel wasn't sure she wanted Orlie to read Mary's letter, but she didn't want to be rude, so she smiled and said, "Let's go sit down, and I'll read Mary's letter out loud."

When they were settled on the back porch steps, Rachel tore open the letter and began to read.

"Dear Rachel: I have some very good news. I'll be coming back to Pennsylvania in a few weeks for—"

Woof! Woof! Woof! Buddy darted onto the porch, swiped his sloppy wet tongue across Rachel's face, and then leaped into Orlie's lap.

Jacob, red-faced and sweating, dropped onto the step below them. "That crazy mutt can sure run fast. I'm all worn out!"

Rachel grunted. "You should get rid of him. He's nothing but trouble."

"No way! Buddy's a nice hund." Jacob rubbed Buddy's ears.

Orlie patted the top of Buddy's head. "I'd never have given him to you if it hadn't been for my *mamm's* [mom's] allergies. I'm glad you were able to take Buddy."

Jacob nodded. "I'm glad Buddy came to live with us.

He's been a good friend to me."

Orlie's head bobbed up and down. "He was a good friend to me, too, and he's also a good watchdog."

"You two can sit here all day talking about that dumm hund if you like, but I'm going inside to tell Mom about Mary's letter." Rachel jumped up and raced into the house, banging the screen door behind her. "I got a letter from Mary!" she hollered as she dashed into the kitchen.

Mom was sitting at the table drinking a cup of tea. She looked up and smiled. "That's nice. What'd she say?"

"She's coming to Pennsylvania!"

"When?"

"I don't know. Thanks to Jacob's dumm hund, I didn't get a chance to finish reading Mary's letter." Rachel dropped into a chair and placed the letter on the table. "I'll finish reading it now though. Would you like me to read it out loud?"

"Jah, why don't you?" Mom's metal-framed glasses slipped to the end of her nose, and she pushed them back in place.

Rachel touched the nosepiece of her own plastic-framed glasses. Then she began to read.

> *Dear Rachel,*
>
> *I have some very good news. I'll be coming back to Pennsylvania in a few weeks for a visit. I'll be with our neighbor, Carolyn, who's coming there to see her daughter who's expecting a baby. Mama will call soon*

to let you know when I'll arrive.

Love, Mary.

Rachel looked at Mom and smiled. "Isn't that the best news?"

Mom patted Rachel's arm. "It certainly is. I know how much you've missed Mary. It will be nice for you girls to be together again."

Rachel wiggled in her chair. "I can hardly wait to see Mary again!"

Mom smiled and stood up. "I'd better check on your baby sister. She should be waking from her nap soon. Then she'll need to be diapered and fed."

Mom hurried from the room, and Rachel picked up Mary's letter to read it again.

Clip-clop. Clip-clop.

Pap's new horse pulled their gray box-shaped buggy down the road the following morning. Rachel and her family were headed to church. It would be held at Howard and Anna Miller's house today.

Rachel enjoyed going to church every other Sunday with her family and friends, and this morning she was even more eager to attend. She wanted to tell her friend Audra Burkholder about her letter from Mary.

When they approached the Millers' barn, Rachel spotted Audra and Orlie across the yard by the swing. As soon as Pap stopped the horse, she hopped out of the buggy and sprinted across the yard.

"Wie geht's? [How are you?]*"* Rachel asked Audra.

"Okay," Audra mumbled; then she quickly looked away.

Rachel looked at Orlie and smiled, but he hurried away. Rachel figured he was going to join some of the boys.

"Guess what?" Rachel asked, nudging Audra's arm.

Audra shrugged.

"I got a letter from—"

"Church is about to begin. We need to get inside." Audra hurried toward the buggy shed, where several wooden benches had been set up for the members of their Amish community to sit on during the three-hour church service.

I guess I'll have to wait until church is over to tell Audra about Mary's letter, Rachel thought. She followed behind the others to the shed, her shoulders slumped and her head dropped in disappointment.

Whoomp! Rachel bumped into Sadie Stoltzfus, a widow. "Oops! I'm sorry," she said.

Sadie turned and scowled at Rachel. "You should watch where you're going. Can't you see that there are people in front of you?" Her false teeth clacked when she spoke.

"I—I was looking at the ground and didn't see you."

Sadie blinked her pale green eyes and shook her

finger. "Well, you should pay more attention. Hasn't your mamm ever told you to hold your head up when you walk?"

Rachel nodded.

"Then you should listen." Sadie's teeth clacked a little louder, and she shook her finger again. "I'm glad all my *kinskinner* [grandchildren] are grown. I have no patience with little *kinner* [children] anymore."

Rachel thought it was obvious that Sadie didn't care much for children. "I'm sorry I bumped into you," she said. Then she hurried into the building.

When Rachel looked at the women's side of the room, she spotted Audra sitting between Phoebe Byler and Karen Fisher. Rachel was disappointed again. She usually sat by Audra. Maybe they could sit together during the noon meal.

Rachel slipped onto a bench beside Rebekah Mast.

As the group began to sing the first song, Rachel looked at Audra and smiled.

Audra stared straight ahead.

Every few minutes Rachel looked at Audra, but Audra never glanced Rachel's way.

Maybe Audra's afraid she'll get in trouble for fooling around in church, Rachel thought. *That's probably why she won't look at me.*

Rachel heard someone clear her throat loudly. She glanced over her shoulder. Sadie Stoltzfus was frowning at Rachel. Rachel turned back around. She was glad she wasn't one of Sadie's kinskinner.

Harvey Fisher, one of the ministers, began giving his sermon, so Rachel sat up straight and listened.

"He who guards his mouth and his tongue keeps himself from calamity," Harvey quoted from Proverbs 21:23.

Rachel was good at spelling, and she knew that another word for *calamity* was *trouble. I have lots of trouble,* she thought. *Trouble seems to find me wherever I go.*

She looked at Audra, but Audra still kept her gaze straight ahead. Rachel frowned. Was trouble brewing with Audra?

When church was over and the noon meal had been served, Rachel looked for Audra. She stopped in her tracks when she saw Audra sitting at a table between Phoebe and Karen.

Is Audra trying to avoid me? Is she mad at me for something? Rachel wondered. *Are those her new best friends?*

Rachel felt like crying. She waited until Audra had finished her lunch; then she stepped up to her and said, "Should we go out to the Millers' barn and play?"

Audra shook her head. "I'm not in the mood."

"Then let's go swing."

"Nope." Audra hurried toward the creek.

Rachel looked after her in dismay. What would she do if Audra didn't want to be her friend anymore? First, she'd lost Mary. Had she lost Audra now, too? Who would she play with? Who would she tell her secrets to? Who would be that special friend to laugh with her?

Tears trickled down Rachel's face. She quickly wiped them away. It wouldn't do for Orlie or anyone to see her cry.

"Well, if she doesn't want to be my friend, that's okay!" she said out loud. As soon as she spoke, she remembered the scripture from the morning. *He who guards his mouth and his tongue keeps himself from calamity.*

Maybe I shouldn't say such things, Rachel thought. In fact, a little something inside Rachel nudged her to go after Audra. She'd try to talk to Audra one more time before she gave up on their friendship.

At the creek, she found Audra sitting on a rock with her arms folded, staring at the water.

Rachel knelt in the grass beside Audra and touched her arm. "I wanted to tell you that—"

Ribbet! Ribbet! A little tree frog jumped out of the grass and landed on Audra's shoulder.

"Eeeek!" Audra leaped to her feet up and hopped up and down. "Get the frog, Rachel! Get the frog off me!"

Rachel plucked the frog from Audra's shoulder and dropped it in the water.

Tears rolled down Audra's flushed cheeks.

Rachel patted her back. "It's okay. Don't cry. The frog's gone now."

Audra pulled away. "I–I'm fine." *Sniff! Sniff!*

"It was just a little tree frog," Rachel said. "It wouldn't hurt you. There's no reason for you to cry."

Audra swiped at the tears running down her cheeks. "I'm not just crying because of the frog."

"Why are you crying?"

"I'm not your best friend anymore."

Rachel tilted her head. "Who says you're not my best friend?"

"Orlie."

Rachel frowned. "Why would Orlie say that?"

"He said you got a letter from your cousin." Audra sniffed a couple more times. "Orlie said Mary's moving back to Pennsylvania, and that she's your best friend."

Rachel could hardly believe Orlie had said those things. Was he trying to cause trouble? Was he mad because she'd called Buddy a dumm hund?

"That's not true," Rachel said. "Mary isn't moving back here. She's only coming for a visit. Orlie didn't even hear all of Mary's letter."

"Really?"

Rachel nodded. "Mary and I used to be best friends, but you're my best friend now." She hugged Audra. "I'm excited for you to meet Mary, and for her to meet you, too."

Audra smiled. "I guess Orlie must have jumped to conclusions."

"What's that mean?" Rachel asked.

"'Jumping to conclusions' is an expression I heard from my mamm," Audra said. "When someone jumps to conclusions, it means they've made a decision without getting all the facts."

Rachel hugged Audra again. "I think Orlie jumped to conclusions as high as that frog jumped."

The girls laughed. Rachel felt so good to be friends with Audra. She didn't dare tell Audra about jumping to her own conclusions.

"As soon as Mary gets here, I'll invite you over to play," Rachel promised.

Audra smiled. "*Danki* [Thanks], Rachel. I'll look forward to that."

Chapter 2

Out of Patience

Rachel hurried to finish the breakfast dishes so she could help Grandpa in the greenhouse. She enjoyed spending time with Grandpa. She also liked being around the plants and flowers.

"Would you hold your baby sister while I go to the garden and pull weeds?" Mom asked Rachel.

"How long do I have to hold her?"

"Until she burps."

Rachel's excitement about going to the greenhouse melted like a brick of ice in the hot sun. "*Ach* [Oh], Mom, you know how long Hannah takes to burp." She motioned to the window. "I promised Grandpa I'd help him in the greenhouse this morning."

Mom draped a piece of cloth over Rachel's shoulder and handed her the baby. "Just keep patting her back. I'm sure she'll burp soon; then you can put her down for a nap and go to the greenhouse."

"All right, Mom." Rachel headed for the living room, patting Hannah's back as she went.

Hannah nuzzled Rachel's neck with her soft, warm nose, but she didn't burp.

Rachel continued to pat Hannah's back. "Hurry up, Hannah. I need to get out to the greenhouse."

"Goo-goo. Gaa-gaa." Hannah drooled on Rachel's neck.

"Yuck!" Rachel used the cloth Mom had draped over her shoulder to wipe the drool away. "You're a cute *boppli* [baby], but you can sure cause trouble sometimes."

"Gaa-gaa," was Hannah's response.

Rachel sat on the sofa and placed Hannah facedown across her knees.

Squeak! Squeak! Rachel reached behind her to find one of Hannah's squeaky toys. She tossed it across the room.

Hannah whimpered.

Rachel patted Hannah's back.

Hannah started to howl.

Rachel sat Hannah up and rubbed her back.

Hannah stopped crying, but still no burp.

"Just when I thought I could have a little time to help Grandpa, I'm stuck with a baby who won't burp," Rachel grumbled.

Is this going to take all day? Rachel thought about turning Hannah upside down to see if that would make her burp, but she'd be in big trouble if Mom caught her.

She placed Hannah on her knee and bounced her up and down.

Hannah giggled, but still no burp. She didn't look sleepy, either.

Hic! Hic! Hic!

"Oh, great," Rachel moaned. "Now you've got the hiccups." She placed Hannah in her cradle, hurried into the kitchen, and filled a baby bottle with water.

When Rachel returned to the living room, Hannah was crying between hiccups.

Rachel picked up the baby, sat on the sofa, and gave Hannah some water.

Hannah spit the water out and hiccuped again.

Rachel gritted her teeth.

"Waaa! Waaa!" Hannah's face turned bright red.

Rachel put the baby over her shoulder and patted her back.

Blurp! Hannah spit up on Rachel's shoulder.

"Ewww!" Rachel wrinkled her nose. She placed Hannah in her cradle, scampered to her room, and changed into a clean dress.

When Rachel returned to the living room, Hannah was crying again. She picked up Hannah and took a seat in the rocking chair. Mom often put the baby to sleep by humming and rocking her. Rachel hoped it would work for her, too.

"Hmm. . .hmm. . .hmm. . ." Rachel hummed while she rocked back and forth.

Hannah continued to fuss and squirm.

"Please go to sleep," Rachel begged. "You should be sleepy by now, Hannah."

"Waaa! Waaa!" Hannah's face turned even redder, and she waved her chubby little hands in the air.

Just then, Rachel felt something damp on her knee. "That's just great," she said with a moan. "Your diaper must be full, and it leaked on my dress."

Rachel placed Hannah in the cradle and quickly changed the wet diaper. It was not her favorite thing to do!

Hannah finally quit crying and fell asleep. Rachel sighed with relief. Then she hurried upstairs to change her dress so she could go to the greenhouse.

As Rachel skipped across the grass toward Grandpa's greenhouse, she felt like she was floating on a cloud. She still couldn't believe Grandpa had put her name under his on the wooden sign outside the greenhouse. She felt good to know that he wanted her help and almost thought of her as his partner.

Rachel shivered as a cool wind blew several leaves across the yard. Summer was nearly over, and soon school would start again. Usually Rachel looked forward to this time of year, but now things were different.

Going back to school would mean less free time to help Grandpa in the greenhouse. Rachel would also have homework every evening.

I won't think about that now, Rachel decided. *I'll just enjoy every day I'm able to work with Grandpa.*

A musty, damp odor met Rachel when she opened the door to the greenhouse. She figured Grandpa must have recently watered the plants.

Rachel looked around but didn't see Grandpa. She decided he was in his office or at the back of the greenhouse where he kept supplies. Sure enough, she found Grandpa pruning a large green plant with pointed leaves.

"I'm sorry for being late, Grandpa." Rachel frowned as she thought about what she'd been through in the last hour. "Mom asked me to burp the boppli, and I had all kinds of trouble."

"That's all right," Grandpa said without looking up.

"What kind of plant are you working on?" Rachel asked.

"This is an ivy plant. It pulls toxins from the air, which helps us breathe better." Grandpa motioned to another plant across the room. "That's a spider plant. It does the same thing."

"I didn't realize plants could clean the air," Rachel said. "Guess I have a lot to learn about greenhouse things."

"You'll learn more as time goes on. It's taken me a whole lifetime to learn what I know." Grandpa's bushy gray eyebrows drew together when he looked at Rachel. "Why are you dressed like that?"

"Like what?"

He motioned to her dress. "It's on backwards."

Rachel touched the neck of her dress and grimaced. "I had to change my dress because Hannah wet on me. I guess I wasn't paying attention. I'd better run back to the house and change it around before someone comes into the greenhouse and sees me wearing my dress backwards."

Grandpa chuckled. "We sure couldn't have that, could we? If someone saw you wearing your dress backwards they might think I hired a *verhuddelt* [mixed-up] girl to work in my greenhouse."

Rachel blushed. "Do you really think I'm verhuddelt?"

Grandpa hugged her. "Of course not. I just think you get in too big of a hurry sometimes instead of being patient."

Rachel nodded. "I get frustrated when I have to wait for things."

"One of my favorite Bible verses is Psalm 40:1: 'I waited patiently for the Lord.' You should think about that whenever you feel impatient." Grandpa squeezed Rachel's shoulder. "Now run into the house and turn your dress around; then hurry back here so we can play with some plants."

"I'll be back as quick as I can." She hugged Grandpa and scurried out the door.

When Rachel entered the house, she was relieved to see that Hannah was still asleep, and Mom was taking a nap on the sofa. She didn't want Mom to see her dress.

Rachel scrambled up the steps. "The hurrier I go, the behinder I get," she mumbled. It was one of Grandpa's favorite sayings.

She zipped into her room, slipped off her dress, and put it back on the right way. Then she scurried out of the room, dashed down the stairs, and raced out the back door.

She'd just stepped off the porch when she spotted her English friend Sherry coming up the driveway. Sherry had her fluffy little dog, Bundles, on a leash.

"Hi, Rachel." Sherry waved. "I came over to see if you could play."

"I can't today. I'm supposed to help my grandpa in his greenhouse," Rachel said as she hurried to meet Sherry.

"Oh, that's right." Sherry pointed to the greenhouse. "I still haven't seen it inside. Can I look at it now?"

"I'd be happy to show you around." Rachel pointed at the dog. "Bundles will have to stay outside, though. Grandpa doesn't allow animals in the greenhouse. Whenever they've gotten in by mistake, there's been trouble."

"Okay." Sherry tied Bundles's leash to a fence post. Bundles plopped on the ground and closed her eyes.

At least she's not the kind of dog who barks a lot, jumps up, and licks you, Rachel thought. Sherry's sweet little dog was nothing like Jacob's troublesome mutt.

Sherry pointed to the sign above the greenhouse door. "I didn't know you owned this place, too."

Rachel shook her head. "Grandpa's the legal owner. I help him here whenever I can, so he included my name on the sign."

"Maybe you'll own it someday—after your grandpa's too old to work anymore."

"I hope that won't be for a long time." Rachel opened the door. She didn't see any sign of Grandpa and figured he was probably in the back room repotting or pruning plants.

"This place is great! There are so many pretty plants and flowers, and it smells good," Sherry said. "My mom's birthday's in a few weeks. Maybe I'll buy a plant for her."

Rachel nodded. "I'm sure she'd like that."

Zzzz. . . Zzzz. . .

Sherry tipped her head. "What's that weird noise?"

Rachel listened to the low rumble coming from the back room. "I think it's my grandpa snoring. He must have fallen asleep. He's quite a *schnarixer* [snorer]."

"What's a schnarixer?" Sherry asked.

"It means 'snorer,'" Rachel explained.

Sherry snickered. "My dad's a schnarixer, too."

Rachel chuckled. "My brother's dog sometimes snores. When he does, he sounds like a freight train."

Woof! Woof!

Rachel glanced out the window. "It looks like something's upset your dog; she's barking and tugging on her leash."

Sherry flipped her blond ponytail. "Guess I'd better get out there and see what's riled Bundles."

Rachel followed Sherry out the door. She saw Snowball, one of Cuddles's kittens, prancing around with her tail lifted, just out of Bundles's reach.

"Come here, you silly *bussli* [kitten]." Rachel was about to pick Snowball up when the kitten leaped into the air and landed on Bundles's head.

Woof! Woof! Bundles shook her head, tossing Snowball into a clump of bushes.

Meow!

Rachel gasped. "Snowball! Oh, you poor little thing. Are you hurt?"

She couldn't see the kitten. She only heard a pitiful *Meow!* coming from inside the bushes.

"She probably won't come out as long as your dog's here," Rachel told Sherry.

Sherry nodded. "I'd better head for home."

"What about the plant for your mother?"

"I'll come back another day and pick one out."

Sherry scooped up her dog. "I'm sorry for all the trouble, Rachel."

"It's okay. Snowball shouldn't have been teasing Bundles." Rachel glanced at the bushes. "I wish she'd come out, though."

"I'm sure she will once we're gone." Sherry squeezed Rachel's arm. "I'll come over to get the plant soon, and I'll leave Bundles at home."

As Sherry hurried away, Rachel leaned into the bushes and called, "Here Snowball. It's safe to come out now."

No response. Not even a meow.

Rachel pulled the bushes apart and spotted a fluffy white tail. "Come here, you silly bussli."

Snowball swished her tail and went deeper into the bushes.

Rachel stuck her hand inside the bush. She felt around until she touched a soft furry paw.

"Yeow!" Snowball scratched Rachel's hand with her sharp little claws and flew out of the bushes.

Rachel turned to chase after the kitten, but her sleeve caught on the bush. *Rip!* A hunk of material tore loose.

"Trouble, trouble, trouble!" Back to the house Rachel stomped, grumbling and mumbling all the way.

She zipped up the stairs, raced into her room, and flopped onto the bed. This had not been a good morning! Now she really was out of patience!

Chapter 3

Eavesdropping

When Rachel returned to the greenhouse, she was surprised to see Grandpa standing on his head in one corner of the greenhouse.

"*Was in der welt* [What in all the world] are you doing?" she asked, bending down to see Grandpa's face.

"My brain felt foggy," Grandpa said. "I'm letting the blood run to my head so I can think better."

Rachel stared at Grandpa and slowly shook her head. She could hardly believe a man his age was strong enough to stand on his head.

"I've been doing this since I was a *buwe* [boy]," Grandpa said. "I could stand on my head longer than any of my *brieder* [brothers]." He lowered his feet to the floor and slowly stood.

Rachel wondered how many other things Grandpa could do that she didn't know about.

"You sure took a long time turning your dress

around," Grandpa said. He studied Rachel. "Say, that's not the same dress you were wearing earlier. Your backwards dress was blue, and this one's green."

"This is the second time I've changed my dress," Rachel said. "Well, really the third time, since the baby wet on my other dress. Oh, and I had another dress before that—until Hannah spit up on it."

Grandpa frowned. "I don't remember you going up to the house more than once."

Rachel told him that her friend Sherry had come over. "I showed her the greenhouse. And we heard you snore," she added.

Grandpa puckered his lips and tugged his long beard. "Was I really snoring?"

"Jah."

"Guess I must have fallen asleep at my desk." Grandpa chuckled. "Your grandma never got used to my snoring. She told our kinner, 'When he snores, he keeps me awake.'"

A look of sadness spread over Grandpa's face, but he quickly covered it with a smile.

Rachel knew Grandpa must still miss Grandma, who had gone to heaven several years earlier. "Since my room's upstairs and yours is downstairs, your snoring never keeps me awake," Rachel said, hoping to change the subject. "I sure can't say that about baby Hannah. She keeps me awake when she cries at night."

Grandpa nodded. "I know what you mean. I finally bought myself a pair of earplugs."

"Maybe I should get some, too." Rachel frowned. "But if I had earplugs, I might not hear my alarm clock ring when school starts next month."

Grandpa tweaked the end of Rachel's nose. "That wouldn't be good, now, would it?"

She shook her head. "Guess I'll have to put up with Hannah's crying until she grows out of it."

"At the rate the boppli's growing, she'll soon sleep all night."

Grandpa pointed to some potted plants on a nearby shelf. "I watered a few of those plants earlier, but I have some office work to do, so why don't you water the plants over there?" He pointed to some plants on the other side of the room.

"Okay." Rachel hurried to the sink, filled the watering can, and headed to a tray of purple and white petunias. She'd just started back across the room for more water when the greenhouse door swung open.

"*Guder mariye* [Good morning]," their neighbor Anna Miller said when she stepped inside.

"Guder mariye," Rachel said with a smile.

"Is your grandpa here?" Anna asked.

Rachel motioned to the small room Grandpa used as his office. "He's at his desk, but you can go in if you like."

"Danki." Anna headed for the office, and Rachel scurried to the sink. As she carried the watering can back across the room, she noticed a praying mantis sitting on the shelf between two pots of pansies.

Rachel watched as it devoured a fly, one limb at a time. Rachel didn't care much for dirty flies, but she almost felt sorry for this one because it had no chance to get away.

"It's sure. . . A worm. . ."

"Jah, that's right. . . . It's kind of. . ."

Rachel listened to Grandpa's and Anna's voices. She figured Grandpa must have spotted a worm someplace, which was strange, since he had no plants in his office.

"It wouldn't be so bad. . .Wasn't full of humility. . ."

Rachel set the watering can down. She eased closer to the office door to better hear what they were saying.

"I can't really blame her. . ."

"I know what you mean. . ."

Rachel put her ear against the door. She wished they would talk a little louder.

Suddenly the door swung open, knocking Rachel to the floor.

"Ach, Grandpa, you scared me!" She scrambled to her feet.

Grandpa stepped toward Rachel. "Are you all right?"

"I—I'm fine. It just knocked the wind out of me when you opened the door."

Grandpa frowned. "Why were you by the door? I thought you were watering plants."

Rachel's face warmed with embarrassment. "I—I was, but I heard you and Anna talking about a worm, and—" She glanced over her shoulder. "Is there a worm in your office, Grandpa?"

He shook his head. "Of course not. I don't know where you got such a notion. I never said anything about a worm."

"He said it's a *warm* day. Maybe that's what you heard," Anna said, entering the main part of the greenhouse. "And I said, 'It wouldn't be so bad if it wasn't for the humidity.' "

"I thought you said 'humility,' " Rachel said.

Anna shook her head. "No. Never said a word about humility."

Rachel stared at the floor. She felt foolish.

Grandpa frowned. "I think you'd better get back to work and stop eavesdropping, Rachel."

"Okay." Rachel shuffled back to finish watering the plants.

As Grandpa and Anna continued their conversation, Rachel tried not to listen. It was hard, though, because she was sure they were talking about interesting things.

"I think an African violet would be a perfect plant for her," Grandpa said.

Perfect plant for who? Rachel wanted to ask, but she

knew Grandpa wouldn't appreciate her listening to his conversation again.

"Jah, I'm sure she'll like the plant, and I think. . ." Anna's voice trailed off as she moved to the other side of the room.

Rachel wished she could follow, but she had more plants to water.

"That's right; it's not good to be alone. I'm sure you must miss. . ."

Rachel tipped her head and strained to hear the rest of what Anna was saying.

"Marriage is. . ." Anna moved even farther away, and then her voice sounded like a whisper.

Rachel gritted her teeth. She couldn't hear any of Anna's words now.

She raced to the sink, filled the watering can with more water, and started watering plants closer to where Grandpa and Anna stood.

"Thanks for stopping by, Anna," Grandpa said. "When you see Sadie Stoltzfus, tell her I'll be over later today. I need to ask her that question."

Rachel's ears perked up. Why would Grandpa go to see the widow Stoltzfus, who didn't like kids and clacked her false teeth?

Anna paused and smiled at Grandpa. "A fall wedding will be nice, don't you think?"

He nodded, and Anna hurried out the door.

Jumping to Conclusions: *Rachel Yoder—Always Trouble Somewhere*

Rachel stood like a statue in front of the flowers, her mouth hanging open. This couldn't happen! No, it just couldn't!

Grandpa nudged Rachel's arm. "What are you doing? Catching flies?"

"Huh?"

"Your mouth's hanging open. I wondered if you were trying to catch a few flies."

Rachel clamped her mouth shut. Her hand shook so badly that some water sloshed out of the watering can and landed on her bare foot.

Grandpa snickered. "Now what are you doing— giving yourself a bath?"

Rachel tried to swallow around the lump in her throat. She couldn't tell Grandpa what had upset her. If she said what she'd heard, he would know she'd been listening to his and Anna's conversation.

"I—uh—guess I wasn't watching what I was doing," she mumbled.

He patted her arm. "If you're done watering, I'd like you to put the watering can away and help me repot some plants that have grown too big for their containers."

Rachel nodded. "I will. . .just as soon as I wipe up the water I spilled."

As Rachel hurried to get a clean rag, she made a decision. She would have to find a way to keep Grandpa

42

from marrying Sadie Stoltzfus!

By the time Rachel had watered all the plants and helped Grandpa repot several, it was time to go to the house and help Mom make lunch.

Rachel had just started across the yard when she spotted Jacob coming around the side of the barn.

"I'm so glad you're here," she said breathlessly. "I need to talk to you."

Jacob eyed her with a curious expression. "What about?"

"Grandpa's on the verge of making the biggest mistake of his life. He's not thinking straight. He needs our help to. . ."

Jacob held up his hand. "Slow down, Rachel. You're talking way too fast."

She shook her head. "No, I'm not. You're listening too slow."

He glared at her. "I'm not listening too slow."

Any other time Rachel might have argued, but right now she needed his help more than she needed to prove she was right.

"Grandpa's planning to take a plant over to Sadie Stoltzfus this afternoon," she said.

"How do you know?"

"I heard him tell Anna Miller."

"So what if he's taking a plant to Sadie? She lives

several miles away. It's probably hard for her to hitch the horse to the buggy and travel to Grandpa's greenhouse," Jacob said.

Rachel lowered her voice. "He's not just taking Sadie a plant. He's getting married again."

Jacob raised his eyebrows. "Who's he going to marry?"

Rachel groaned. "Aren't you listening? I'm talking about the Widow Stoltzfus! When he takes her the African violet, Grandpa's going to ask her to marry him."

Jacob's eyes widened. "Are you sure?"

"Of course I'm sure. I was in the greenhouse when Anna and Grandpa were talking about Sadie Stoltzfus. They talked about a wedding in the fall and about Grandpa needing a wife." Rachel drew in a quick breath. "He said he's going to see Sadie later today, to take her a plant and ask her a question."

Jacob slowly shook his head. "You're *an lauerer* [eavesdropper], Rachel. You should quit nosing around and mind your own business."

Rachel stomped her foot. "If we don't do something to stop it, we'll end up with a new teeth-clacking *grossmudder* [grandmother] who doesn't like kinner!"

"This is none of our business, Rachel. If Grandpa wants to marry her, that's his decision. You need to keep your nose out of Grandpa's business and spend your time doing something else." He poked her arm. "Maybe you should get busy and clean your room so it'll be ready when Cousin Mary gets here."

"I've been getting ready for Mary, but she won't be here for a week or so." Rachel pursed her lips. "Right now we need to concentrate on—"

"Listening to other people's conversations can lead to trouble," Jacob interrupted. "Besides, you don't even know if you heard correctly."

Rachel knew all about trouble. It seemed to follow her everywhere.

She squinted her eyes at Jacob and said, "If I did hear correctly, then we need to do something to stop it!"

Jacob shook his head. "That wouldn't be right. If Grandpa wants to marry again, you should be happy for him."

Tears welled in Rachel's eyes. "I—I can't be happy about this. If Grandpa marries Sadie, he'll move out of our house, and she'll—"

"How do you know Sadie won't move in with us?"

Rachel gasped. "Do you really think she might do that?"

Jacob shrugged. "All I know is whatever Grandpa does, it's his business, not ours." He walked toward the house. "I don't know about you, but I'm hungry. I'm going inside to eat lunch!"

Rachel sighed. She'd hoped she could count on Jacob,

but he'd been no help at all! If anything was going to be done to keep Grandpa from marrying Sadie Stoltzfus, she'd have to do it alone!

Chapter 4
Busybody

"Rachel, why aren't you eating your lunch?" Mom asked, nodding at the half-eaten peanut butter and jelly sandwich on Rachel's plate. "Aren't you hungry this afternoon?"

Rachel shrugged. "I have a lot on my mind."

Jacob snickered. "She's probably thinking up some kind of trouble to get into."

Rachel glared at Jacob. "Am not."

"I'll bet you are, little *bensel* [silly child]."

"Oh, quit your jabbering. I'm not a silly child!"

"Jah, you are."

Pap loudly cleared his throat. "That'll be enough, Jacob! Leave your *schweschder* [sister] alone and finish eating your lunch so we can get back to the fields."

"That's right," Rachel's older brother Henry said. "We have a lot of work to do out there yet today."

Jacob grabbed his sandwich and took a big bite.

Rachel did the same. She knew if she didn't finish her lunch, Mom probably wouldn't let her go back to the greenhouse. She needed to go out there so she could talk Grandpa out of going to see Sadie! She had to make him realize that Sadie wasn't the right woman for him to marry.

Rachel wondered if she should say something to her folks about Grandpa marrying Sadie Stoltzfus.

I'd better not, she decided. *If Grandpa hasn't told them, he might not like it if I blab.*

Rachel crumpled her napkin into a tight little ball. *I wonder why Grandpa told Anna Miller about his plans. I don't think he would have said anything to Anna if he didn't want Mom and Pap to know.*

Rachel knew that Anna was one of Mom's best friends. The next time Anna saw Mom, she was bound to say something about Grandpa getting married. Maybe it would be best to let Anna tell. Then Rachel wouldn't get into trouble for listening to Grandpa and Anna's conversation. When Mom heard the news from Anna, she might convince Grandpa that he was doing the wrong thing by marrying Sadie. After all, Grandpa was Mom's dad, and she probably wouldn't like the idea of him getting married again—especially not to a cranky old woman!

"Sure hope we get the rest of the hay cut today," Pap said before picking up his glass to take a drink.

Henry nodded. "If we can keep my little *bruder* [brother] working this afternoon, we should be able to get it done."

Jacob frowned at Henry. "I always work hard; you know I do!"

Henry thumped Jacob's back. "Jah, most of the time."

"You'd better all work hard this afternoon," Grandpa said, "because some rain is heading our way." He pulled his fingers through the ends of his beard and nodded. "Maybe tonight, maybe tomorrow, but I know it's coming."

"How do you know?" Jacob asked.

Grandpa rubbed his hands over his arms. "I feel it in my bones. They always ache a bit when rain is coming."

"It's true," said Mom. "Even when I was a *maedel* [girl] my *daed* [dad] could forecast the weather by the way he felt in his bones." She frowned. "If we're going to have rain, I hope it holds off until I weed my garden."

"If you need help with that, let me know," Grandpa said with a smile. "When I'm not busy with customers in the greenhouse, I'd be happy to help pull a few weeds."

"I'd appreciate that," Mom said. "It's been hard to keep up with the weeds this summer. They've been growing too fast. Of course," she added, "Hannah's growing nearly as fast. She can no longer wear the outfit I brought her home from the hospital in."

Pap chuckled. "You're right, Miriam. Why, it won't

be long until our little girl will be all grown up and running around this place causing all kinds of trouble."

"Just like Rachel. Always trouble somewhere, right, Rachel?" Jacob jabbed Rachel's arm just as she was about to drink her milk.

Whoosh! Milk sloshed out of Rachel's glass, trickled down her chin, and splashed onto the front of her dress.

Rachel opened her balled-up napkin and blotted her dress; then she frowned at Jacob and said, "You did that on purpose, didn't you?"

He shook his head. "Did not. How was I to know you were going to pick up your glass?"

"You shouldn't have poked your sister's arm," Pap scolded. "You should keep your hands to yourself. Now tell Rachel you're sorry."

"Sorry," Jacob mumbled.

Rachel didn't think Jacob looked one bit sorry, but she figured Pap would scold her if she didn't accept Jacob's apology. Without looking at Jacob, she said, "You're forgiven."

"Nothing's more beautiful than watching a woman do her work," Grandpa said as he and Rachel repotted a large split-leafed plant in his greenhouse that afternoon.

Rachel smiled. It made her feel good to be called a woman, even though she still had several more birthdays before she'd really be one. At least Grandpa didn't think of her as a little girl anymore.

That was more than she could say for Jacob. Every chance he got he reminded her that she was two years younger than he was. His constant teasing made her feel like a little girl. She hoped he would stop calling her a little bensel. It would be embarrassing if he still called her that when she was a grown woman.

Rachel glanced over at Grandpa. Since he hadn't said a word about going to see Sadie Stoltzfus, she hoped he'd changed his mind. Maybe he'd had time to think things through and realized that Sadie wouldn't be a good wife for him.

"Are you getting excited about Mary coming to visit?" Grandpa asked, smiling at Rachel.

Rachel nodded. "Oh jah. I'm very excited!"

"I imagine you two will have lots to talk about—lots of catching up to do."

"You're right about that." Rachel grinned. "I can hardly wait to show her the bussli Mom let me keep from Cuddles's litter of kittens."

"I'm sure the two of you will have lots of fun." Grandpa pulled the sack of potting soil closer to them, scooped out some dirt, and poured it into the empty pot. "Are you looking forward to going back to school next month?"

Rachel dug her shovel into the sack and added some dirt to the pot. "I guess so, but I'll miss working here every day."

"You can work after school and on Saturdays," he reminded her.

"I know, but it won't be the same."

"Sure it will. You just won't be working here as many hours as you are now." Grandpa placed the plant in the pot and patted the soil around it. "I think we're about done with this. Would you clean up the dirt we've spilled?"

Rachel was pleased that Grandpa had said "we" instead of blaming her for spilling the dirt. Jacob would have blamed her for it if they'd repotted the plant together.

"Jah, sure, I can clean up the dirt." Rachel headed to get the broom and dustpan from the back room.

When Rachel returned, she was surprised to see Grandpa wearing his straw hat.

"I'm going to Sadie Stoltzfus's place with an African violet plant," he said.

Rachel's heart beat faster. She had to think of something to keep Grandpa from going. She couldn't let him propose marriage to Sadie!

"Say, Grandpa," she said, tugging on his shirtsleeve, "I'll take the plant to Sadie! That way you'll be here in case any customers come."

"It's a long walk to Sadie's, Rachel." He smiled and squeezed her arm. "Besides, I think you can handle waiting on customers."

Rachel's mouth went dry. "Ach no! I wouldn't be comfortable here alone for that long."

"I won't be gone long, Rachel. What I have to say to Sadie will only take a few minutes."

Rachel thought for a minute. Was Grandpa going to ask Sadie to marry him and then come right back home? She remembered the evening Rudy had asked Esther to marry him. He'd taken her out for a buggy ride, and they'd been gone a long time. Maybe older folks didn't need such a long time to ask someone to marry them.

"Say, Grandpa," Rachel quickly said, "before you go, could you answer a question for me?"

He nodded. "Make it fast, though. I need to get going."

Rachel pointed to a purple African violet on the shelf across the room. "How come the leaves on that plant are pointing straight up and not out like the others?"

"Because that African violet needs more light." Grandpa handed Rachel the small shovel he'd been holding and headed across the room. "Danki for mentioning it."

He took the plant from the shelf and placed it closer to the window. "You have a good eye for things. I'm glad you're helping me in the greenhouse."

Rachel smiled. She liked to be appreciated for the good things she did. Sometimes she felt as if her family saw only the wrong things she did.

"Guess I'd better head on over to Sadie's now." Grandpa moved toward the door.

Rachel jumped in front of him. "Wait! I have another question."

Grandpa lifted one edge of his straw hat and scratched his forehead. "What is it, Rachel?"

"I've noticed that some African violets have pretty flowers and others don't. Is there a reason why some of them don't have any blooms?"

He nodded. "A plant might not flower for several reasons."

"Like what?"

"It might need more light, a warmer temperature, or a bit more humidity. A special plant food for African violets often helps, too," he said.

"What kind of plant food?" Rachel leaned against the door and gazed at Grandpa. If she could get him talking about plants, he might forget about going to Sadie's.

Grandpa opened a cupboard door and removed a small box. "This is the plant food I'm talking about. It has special nutrients that help a plant produce nice, healthy flowers."

"Hmm. . . That's interesting." Rachel pointed to a miniature rosebush. "Will the same kind of plant food work for that?"

Grandpa shook his head. "African violet food is only for African violet plants." He removed another box from the cupboard. "This plant food is made for roses."

"A person sure needs to know a lot in order to run a greenhouse," Rachel said. "I wonder if I'll ever know as much as you do."

"If you keep helping me out, you'll learn real fast." Grandpa stepped around Rachel and opened the door. "I'm off to see Sadie now. *She dich, eich, wider* [See you later]!" He stepped outside.

Rachel slumped against the wall with a groan. "I'm doomed."

A few seconds later, the greenhouse door opened, and Grandpa stepped back inside. "I forgot the African violet, and I need my umbrella because it's beginning to rain." He hurried across the room and was about to pick up a lacy-leafed pink and white African violet when Rachel rushed forward and grabbed his arm.

"Grandpa, I—"

Thunk! Her hand bumped the pot. The African violet crashed to the floor, crushing the plant and spilling dirt everywhere!

Rachel gasped.

Grandpa moaned.

Both of them stared at the floor.

"I'm sorry, Grandpa," Rachel said. "I didn't mean to bump your arm and make such a mess."

"It's not the mess that upsets me, Rachel." Grandpa slowly shook his head. "This is the last African violet

I have with lacy pink and white edges. Since that's the kind Sadie wants, I'll have to go empty-handed and explain what happened."

Rachel jumped to her feet. "You're going anyway. . . even without the plant?"

He nodded.

"Can't you propose to Sadie some other time? When you get another lacy-leafed pink African violet?"

Grandpa's bushy eyebrows rose. "Propose what, Rachel?"

"Heiraat [marriage]."

He rubbed his forehead. "You think I'm going over to Sadie's to propose marriage to her?"

Rachel nodded as her eyes filled with tears. "I don't want you to marry Sadie, Grandpa. She doesn't like kinner, and she clicks her teeth when she talks."

"Ha-ha! Ho-ho!" Grandpa laughed so hard his face turned bright red and tears rolled down his wrinkled cheeks.

Rachel frowned. She didn't think what she'd said was funny.

When Grandpa finally stopped laughing, he wiped his eyes, walked to Rachel, and bent down to look her right in the eye. "Where in the world did you get the idea that I was planning to marry Sadie Stoltzfus?"

Rachel didn't know what she should say. Grandpa might be mad if she told him the truth.

Grandpa nudged Rachel's arm. *"Raus mitt* [Out with it]*!"*

Rachel blushed as she explained how she'd heard him and Anna talking. She said, "When you said you were going to take a plant over to Sadie and that you needed to ask her a question, I figured you were going to ask her to marry you."

Grandpa frowned. "You shouldn't have eavesdropped, Rachel. That makes you a busybody, you know."

"I—I didn't mean to listen in. I was worried when I thought you'd decided to marry Sadie," Rachel said. "It was just a big *missverschtand* [misunderstanding], and I'm glad I heard wrong." She was glad she hadn't said anything about Grandpa getting married to anyone but Jacob. She'd have to let him know right away that it was a mistake.

"You're right about it being a misunderstanding, Rachel." Grandpa shook his head. "For your information, Anna and I were talking about her nephew getting married. We also discussed Sadie because she'd told Anna that she wanted a lacy-edged pink African violet to give to her sister as a birthday present."

"But I heard you say it wasn't good to be alone, and that you missed Grandma."

"I do still miss your grandma, but you are mistaken about everything else. Anna mentioned that Sadie lived alone and didn't get out much because she couldn't control the horse and buggy. That's why I said I'd take the African violet to her."

Grandpa's forehead wrinkled. "You should never listen to other people's conversations, and you shouldn't assume anything."

"I'm sorry," Rachel mumbled.

"Sorry is good, but you need to learn a lesson from your mistake." Grandpa snapped his fingers and pointed to the floor. "I'll take a different plant to Sadie and explain that the one I'd chosen fell on the floor. While I'm gone, you clean up that mess. Then you can sweep the rest of the rooms."

Rachel nodded and dropped to her knees. It was never fun to be punished, but at least one thing was good: She didn't have to worry about Grandpa marrying Sadie Stoltzfus! She couldn't wait to tell Jacob the good news.

Chapter 5

Tittle-tattle

One week later, Rachel poked her head into the kitchen and spotted Mom sitting at the table, reading the newspaper and drinking a glass of iced tea.

"I was hoping I'd find you here," Rachel said. "I need to ask you about the message you found on our answering machine in the phone shed this morning."

Mom looked up and smiled. "What message? There were several."

"The one from Aunt Irma, about Mary."

"Oh, that." Mom smiled and winked at Rachel. "What do you want to know about Aunt Irma's message that I haven't already told you?"

Rachel pulled out a chair and sat down. "If Mary arrives when her mamm said, then she should be here sometime tomorrow, right?"

Mom nodded. "I imagine you're pretty excited."

"I am, but I'm also kind of *naerfich* [nervous]." Rachel

touched her stomach. "It feels like a bunch of butterflies are zipping around in here."

"Why would you be nervous about Mary coming?" Mom asked.

"What if she doesn't recognize me with my glasses? What if she doesn't like me anymore? What if. . ."

"You're getting yourself all worked up for nothing. You don't look that different with glasses, and I'm sure Mary still likes you. After all, you and Mary have been good friends since you were *bopplin* [babies]." Mom patted Rachel's arm. "Once Mary gets here, I'm sure you'll see that you've worried for nothing."

Rachel nodded. "I hope so."

"Since Grandpa closed the greenhouse today to go fishing, why don't you go visit one of your friends?" Mom suggested. "It might help get your mind off those butterflies in your stomach and keep you from thinking about things that aren't likely to happen."

"I guess I could go to Audra's and see how she's getting along with the kitten I gave her as a birthday present," Rachel said. "I could take Snowball with me, and our kittens could play together."

Mom nodded. "I think that's a *gut* [good] idea. Why don't you get your kitten and head to Audra's right now?"

"Okay, I'll be home in time to help with supper." Rachel raced out the door.

Rachel stepped onto the back porch of Audra's house,

holding her squirming kitten against her chest. "Is anyone home?" she called, peering through the screen door.

No response.

Tap! Tap! Rachel rapped on the door.

Several seconds later she heard a faint, "I'm coming."

Audra's mother, Naomi, came to the door. Her cheeks were red, and a wisp of hair from under her *kapp* [cap] was stuck to her sweaty forehead.

"Oh, it's you, Rachel. I hope you haven't been waiting long." Naomi pushed her hair back in place. "I was in the basement getting some fruit jars."

Rachel shook her head. "I haven't been here long. Is Audra at home? I brought my kitten over so we could play."

"Audra and Brian went out to skateboard awhile ago." Naomi pointed to the big red barn. "They're probably getting on each other's nerves, so I'm sure Audra will be happy to see you."

Rachel smiled. "I'll head to the barn then." She scampered down the porch steps. She was glad to know she wasn't the only one who had trouble with her brother.

When Rachel entered the barn, the sweet smell of hay tickled her nose. She saw Brian riding a skateboard on one side of the barn where a wooden ramp had been built, while Audra sat on a bale of hay, frowning.

"Wie geht's?" asked Rachel as she took a seat beside her friend.

Audra shrugged. "I'd be better if my bruder would give me a turn on my skateboard."

"Doesn't Brian have his own skateboard?" Rachel asked.

"He did, but he lost it." Audra tapped her foot. "At least that's what he says. I wouldn't be surprised if he's just saying that so he can ride the one you gave me. It's a lot faster than his."

Rachel held up her kitten. "I brought Snowball along. Why don't we play with our kittens until Brian gets tired of skateboarding?"

"That's a good idea." Audra glanced around. "Of course I have to find Fluffy first."

"Since Snowball is Fluffy's schweschder, I'll bet Snowball can find her." Rachel placed her kitten on the floor. "Go get her, Snowball! Find Fluffy!"

Audra snickered. "Do you really think that just because they're sisters Snowball can find Fluffy?"

Rachel nodded. "Of course. You know everyone in your family, don't you?"

"Jah, but that's different. We're people and—"

"Look!" Rachel pointed across the room. "Snowball's already found Fluffy, and they're rubbing noses."

Audra smiled. "Say, I have an idea. Why don't we go in the house and make bubble solution? Then we can make lots of bubbles and let our kittens chase them."

"That sounds like fun," Rachel agreed. "Do you have an extra bubble wand for me to use?"

"Of course." Audra grabbed Rachel's hand. "Let's go!"

As Rachel and Audra sat on the back porch blowing bubbles, Snowball and Fluffy zipped across the lawn and leaped into the air, trying to pop the colorful bubbles with their paws.

"This is so much fun! I'm glad you came over," Audra said.

"Me, too." Rachel dipped her wand into the bubble solution and blew. A huge bubble formed, and she blew again, making a second bubble, then a third.

Audra's eyes widened. "How'd you do that?"

"Grandpa taught me. We blow bubbles together whenever we can." Rachel waved her wand in the air, and it blew the triple bubble into the yard. "It just takes a little practice, that's all."

Audra dipped her wand into the bubble solution. She blew and made one bubble, but when she blew again, the first bubble popped. "I think I'd better stick to making one bubble for now."

Rachel set her wand aside and leaned back on her elbows. "Tomorrow will be a big day at our house."

"Why?"

"My cousin Mary's supposed to arrive."

"Oh, that's right; I forgot she was coming to see you soon." Audra set her bubble wand down. "I hope you don't forget about me while your cousin's visiting."

Rachel shook her head. "I told you before that you don't have to worry about losing me as your friend. I still hope you can come over while Mary's there. The three of us can do something fun together."

"Can we jump on your trampoline?"

"Maybe. We can also play at the creek or in the barn."

"I think I'd enjoy jumping on the trampoline most."

"We'll see what Mary wants to do." Rachel noticed that Fluffy and Snowball were lying in the grass, so she stuck the bubble wand in the solution again. "Guess we'd better make some more bubbles for our busslin to chase, because I think they're getting bored."

Audra glanced at the barn. "We may as well, because it doesn't look like Brian will quit skateboarding anytime soon."

"Maybe you should go in and insist that he give it to you," Rachel said. "After all, it's *your* skateboard."

Audra shook her head. "If I did that, he'd keep the skateboard even longer just to make me mad."

Rachel clicked her tongue, the way Mom often did when she was trying to make a point. "Brothers can sure be *peschte* [pests]."

"I agree." Audra blew another bubble and sent it

sailing across the yard. "My bruder is the worst pescht of all!" She wrinkled her nose. "There's something else I can tell you about Brian."

"What's that?"

Audra leaned closer to Rachel and whispered, "He sometimes wets the bed."

Rachel gasped. "That's *baremlich* [terrible]!" She was glad no one in her family wet the bed. That would be so embarrassing!

When Rachel arrived home that afternoon, she raced into the house. "Mom, I'm back!"

Mom stepped out of the kitchen, holding a squirming, fussy baby. "Did you have a good time at Audra's?" she asked, raising her voice above Hannah's cries.

Rachel nodded. "But we never got to use Audra's skateboard because Brian hogged it the whole time I was there."

Mom placed Hannah against her shoulder and patted her back. Rachel was glad when the baby stopped crying.

"Did Audra tell her mamm that Brian wouldn't share?" Mom asked, sitting at the table.

Rachel shook her head. "Audra knew if she did that, then Brian would call her a *retschbeddi* [tattletale]."

"Sometimes it's necessary to tell on someone for their misdeeds," Mom said.

Rachel flopped into the chair beside Mom. "If I had a bruder like Brian I'd probably tell on him all of the time." She leaned closer to Mom. "Do you know what Audra told me?"

"Rachel, I don't think—"

"She said Brian sometimes wets the bed." Rachel wrinkled her nose. "Isn't that awful, Mom? Aren't you glad none of your kinner wets the bed?" She pointed to Hannah. "Except for the boppli, of course."

Mom slowly shook her head. "Rachel, you're being a tittle-tattle."

"What's a tittle-tattle?" Rachel asked.

"It's someone who likes to gossip. It seems to me that you like talking about other people and their problems. Bed-wetting is something Brian will outgrow, and you shouldn't make fun of him." Mom tapped Rachel's arm. "Especially since you've wet the bed yourself."

Rachel's face felt hot. "I don't wet the bed!"

"Not anymore, but you did until you turned five."

"I—I don't remember doing that."

"Well, it's true, and no one in our family made fun of you or told anyone else about it." Mom tapped Rachel's arm again. "You need to be careful not to gossip to anyone about Brian's problem, because someone might make fun of him if you do."

"I won't say a word," Rachel said.

Chapter 6
The Big Day

When Rachel awoke the following morning, she felt like singing at the top of her lungs: "Mary's coming today, and I just can't wait!"

Rachel leaped out of bed, rushed to the window, and lifted the shade. No sign of any car or van in the driveway. Mom had said last night that Mary and her neighbor would probably spend the night at a hotel between Indiana and Pennsylvania. Most likely they wouldn't get here until later today. Even so, Rachel wanted to be ready for Mary's arrival, so she hurried to get dressed and raced down the stairs.

She was almost to the bathroom when the door swung open and Pap stepped out.

"I'm surprised to see you up so early." He tapped the top of Rachel's head. "Did you get up at the crack of dawn to help me do my chores?"

Rachel shook her head and bounced up and down

on her toes. "Mary's coming today. I wanted to be sure everything's ready."

"Oh, that's right. Today's the big day." Pap patted Rachel's head again. "It'll probably be several hours before Mary arrives, so calm down and try to relax."

Rachel touched her stomach. It felt like hundreds of butterflies were zipping around again. "I'll try to relax, but it won't be easy."

"If you need something to keep your mind busy, why don't you get breakfast started?" Pap suggested.

Rachel glanced down the hall at her parents' bedroom door. "Isn't Mom getting up?"

"She was up with the boppli several times last night, so I told her to stay in bed awhile longer." Pap motioned to the kitchen. "If you're hungry, you can start breakfast now."

Rachel shook her head. "You know I don't cook well."

"Then why don't you come to the barn and help me?" he suggested.

"What about Jacob and Henry? Aren't they helping?"

"They're in the milking shed, milking the cows."

"Okay," Rachel said with a nod. "As soon as I'm done in the bathroom I'll come to the barn."

When Rachel entered the barn a short time later, she was greeted by the gentle nicker of the horses in their stalls. She spotted Pap across the room, lifting a bale of hay into a large wheelbarrow.

"I'm here, Pap," she called. "What do you need me to do?"

"Why don't you get the hose and give the horses some water while I feed them?"

"Sure, I can do that." Rachel raced to the water faucet and turned on the hose. She was getting ready to haul it to one of the horse's stalls when Pap hollered, *"Bass uff, as du net fallscht* [Take care you don't fall]*! That floor can get slippery when hay mixes with water."

"I'll be care—" *Whoosh!* Rachel's foot hit a wet spot, and down she went!

"Always trouble somewhere," Rachel grumbled as she scrambled to her feet.

Pap raced across the room. "Are you okay? Did you hurt yourself?"

"I'm okay, but my dress got a little wet."

"Next time put the hose in the trough first and then turn on the water. You should have known better than to do something like that," Pap scolded.

Rachel's face heated up. "I was going to fill the horse's trough, but I slipped on the water coming from the hose. I figured I could save time if I turned on the hose first."

"Saving time isn't always the best way to do something," Pap said.

Rachel nodded; then she hurried into the nearest

horse's stall and filled the trough with water. When it was full, she pulled the hose into the next stall. While she watered the horses, she and Pap chatted.

When Rachel was done, she left the hose in one of the troughs, ran back to the faucet, turned off the water, and put the hose away.

"I think I'll go to the house and see if Mom's up," Rachel told Pap.

He nodded. "That's fine. I'll be in shortly."

Before Rachel left the barn, she stopped to pet Cuddles and Snowball, who were sleeping in a pile of hay.

Cuddles purred. Snowball batted Rachel's hand.

"Abastz!" Rachel scolded. "Stop scratching me!"

Meow! Snowball looked at Rachel as if to say, *I'm sorry*.

Rachel stroked the cats until they went back to sleep; then she hurried out of the barn.

Rachel found Mom in the kitchen, stirring a pot of oatmeal. The sweet smell of cinnamon and butter made Rachel's stomach rumble.

Grandpa sat in a chair near the stove, holding Hannah and humming as he stroked her blond hair.

Mom's glasses had fallen to the middle of her nose, and she pushed them back in place as she looked at Rachel. "Where have you been? When I called you to help with breakfast, you weren't in your room."

"I helped Pap with the animals," Rachel said. "I put water in the horses' troughs."

Grandpa pointed to Rachel's dress. "Looks like you watered yourself some, too."

"I fell, but I didn't get hurt, and only a little of my dress got wet." Rachel didn't explain that she'd been dragging the hose across the floor with the water running. She figured she would get a lecture if she mentioned that. "Should I set the table?"

Mom nodded. "When you finish, you can step onto the porch and ring the dinner bell so the menfolk will know breakfast is ready."

"Okay." Rachel hummed as she placed the silverware on the table; then she raced out the door and rang the bell. *Ding! Ding! Ding!*

"Someone's in a good mood this morning," Grandpa said when Rachel returned.

"Mary's coming today. I can hardly wait to see her!" Rachel grinned. "I've got so much to say to Mary!"

"She'll be here for a whole week," Mom said. "You'll have plenty of time to visit."

Pap, Henry, and Jacob entered the kitchen.

"Is breakfast ready?" Jacob asked as he hung his straw hat on a wall peg near the door. "Milkin' cows is hard work, and I'm hungry as a mule!"

"You're not the only one who worked hard this morning." Pap winked at Rachel. "Rachel helped me care for the horses, and *mir hen die zeit verbappelt* [we talked away the time]."

Jacob rolled his eyes. "I can imagine. Rachel's such a blabbermouth; I'll bet she talked your head off."

Rachel glared at Jacob. "I did not. I only talked a little while I watered the horses."

"Don't let Jacob ruffle your feathers." Henry nudged Jacob's arm. "He just likes to see if he can rile you, Rachel."

Rachel shrugged. "No one can rile me this morning."

Jacob tickled Rachel under her chin. "You don't think so? I'll bet I can find a way to rile you."

She pushed his hand away. "You do and I'll rile you right back."

"That'll be enough," Mom said as she placed the pot of oatmeal on the table. She took the baby from Grandpa. "Since Hannah's fallen asleep, I'll put her in the cradle, and then we can eat."

When breakfast was over and the dishes were done, Rachel went outside and sat on the porch swing. *Squeak. . . Squeak. . .Squeak. . .* She pushed her feet against the porch floor to move the swing faster.

"Aren't you coming to the greenhouse this morning?" Grandpa asked when he stepped onto the porch.

Rachel shook her head. "I need to wait for Mary."

"You can wait for her in the greenhouse as well as

you can out here," Grandpa said. "Since you don't know what time she'll arrive, you may as well do something constructive while you wait."

Rachel sighed. She knew Grandpa was right, but it would be hard to do anything when she could only think about when Mary might arrive.

"Well, what do you say?" Grandpa grabbed the armrest of the swing, and it slowed. "Are you coming to the greenhouse with me?"

"I guess so." Rachel hopped off the swing and was about to step off the porch when a van pulled into the yard. It stopped near the house, and a young Amish girl stepped out.

"Mary!" Rachel raced to hug her cousin.

"It's good to see you," Mary said. "I think you've grown a few *zoll* [inches] since I moved."

"You've grown taller, too," Rachel said.

Mary stared at Rachel with a strange expression. "Wow, you sure look different with your new glasses."

Rachel touched the frame of her glasses. "Do—do you think I look weird?"

Mary shook her head. "Of course not. I think you look grown-up."

Rachel sighed with relief. She guessed she'd been worried for nothing.

She grabbed Mary's hands, and the girls twirled in a circle until Rachel felt dizzy. Then she drew in a deep breath. "We're gonna have so much fun while you're here! I have so much to show you and tell you!"

Rachel gulped in another breath. "There's Cuddles's kitten, Snowball; Grandpa's new greenhouse; my baby sister, Hannah; and—"

Woof! Woof! Buddy bounded up to them with a bone in his mouth. *Crackle! Crackle! Crunch! Crunch!* He dropped the bone on the ground and—*slurp!*—licked Rachel's hand.

Rachel pushed him away. "Do you remember this big, hairy mutt of Jacob's?"

Mary giggled and patted Buddy's head. "Jah, and he's still a friendly hund."

Rachel groaned. "Sometimes he's too friendly, and he likes to give big, sloppy, wet kisses!"

Mary patted Buddy's head again. "I like him. He is a nice hund."

"You wouldn't like him if he gave you sloppy kisses all the time!" Rachel grabbed Mary's hand. "Come with me to the barn and I'll show you Cuddles's kitten."

Mary looked at the van. "I need to get my suitcase."

"I'll take care of that," Grandpa said. "I'd like to meet your neighbor and thank her for bringing you here."

Mary opened the van door and introduced Rachel and Grandpa to Carolyn Freeburg. Then Grandpa invited Carolyn to the house to meet Mom.

"Maybe we should go with them," Mary said.

"Not 'til I've shown you the kitten." Rachel nudged Mary's arm, but Mary didn't move.

"I think I should go inside first and say hi to your mamm." Mary darted away before Rachel could respond.

Rachel followed slowly, kicking every pebble she could find. Didn't Mary even care about seeing Cuddles's cute kitten?

By the time Rachel entered the kitchen, Mary was already there. She sat in a chair beside Mom, wearing a satisfied smile and holding Hannah.

"Your little sister's sure cute," Mary said, looking at Rachel. "Makes me wish my mamm would have another boppli."

Rachel shrugged. "Hannah is cute, but she cries a lot."

"Only when she's hungry or needs her *windel* [diaper] changed." Mom stroked the top of Hannah's head.

Grandpa and Carolyn stepped into the room. "Miriam, this is Mary's neighbor, Carolyn Freeburg," he said to Mom.

Mom shook Carolyn's hand. "It's nice to meet you. If you'll have a seat at the table, I'll fix us all some refreshments."

Carolyn smiled. "That's kind of you, Miriam, but please don't go to any trouble on my account."

"It's no trouble at all," Mom said. "I was planning to

give the girls some lemonade and ginger cookies. This will give us all the chance to sit and visit."

Rachel sighed. If they took time to eat cookies, she and Mary would never get to the barn.

"A glass of lemonade does sound good," Carolyn said. "It's turning into a warm, sticky day." She smiled at Mom. "Can I do anything to help?"

"No, no, just have a seat. My daughter will help me get the refreshments." Mom looked at Rachel and said, "Would you please get out the lemonade and paper cups while I put some cookies on a plate?"

Rachel left her seat to do as Mom asked, while Carolyn and Grandpa sat at the table.

When the cookies and lemonade were handed out, Rachel and Mom sat down. Mom asked Carolyn questions about Indiana. Mary continued to play with the baby while Grandpa leaned back in his chair and closed his eyes. Rachel fought the urge to chew on her fingernails. She wanted to show Mary so much, and here they were wasting time at the table!

Finally, Carolyn stood. "I'd best be on my way now. I'm anxious to see my daughter and her baby boy." She patted Mary's shoulder. "Have a good time. I'll be back next week to pick you up."

Mary nodded. "I'll be ready to go when you get here."

Grandpa opened his eyes, yawned, and stood. "Guess I'd better head to my greenhouse and get to work." He patted Rachel's head. "Since Mary's here, I don't expect you to help me today, but you can show her around the greenhouse if you like."

Rachel nodded. "I will after we go to the barn to see Cuddles and Snowball."

"All right. I'll see you two later." Grandpa pulled his straw hat onto his head and went out the door.

"You'll have to give the boppli to my mamm so we can go to the barn," Rachel told Mary.

Mary frowned. "Can't we stay here longer? Hannah's so sweet and cuddly. I like holding her."

"You can hold the boppli later." Rachel started across the room but turned back around. "Are you coming, Mary?"

"Jah, okay." Mary handed the baby to Mom; then she followed Rachel out the door.

Rachel took Mary's hand, and they skipped across the yard.

When they entered the barn, Rachel called, "Here, Cuddles! Here, Snowball! Come out, wherever you are!"

No response. Not even a meow.

"Where are those silly cats?" Rachel ran around the barn, calling the cats and searching the obvious places. She still found no sign of Cuddles or Snowball.

Finally, Rachel turned to Mary and said, "They must be outside. I guess we can look for them after I show you the greenhouse."

"That's fine. I'm anxious to see it," Mary said eagerly.

When they stepped inside the greenhouse a few minutes later, Mary's eyes widened. "Oh, how beautiful! I've never seen so many flowers and plants in one place!"

"Haven't you ever visited a greenhouse?" Grandpa asked.

Mary shook her head. "If you're not too busy, can you show me around?"

Grandpa grinned and tugged his beard. "Since I have no customers right now, I'd be happy to give you a tour of the place."

Rachel gritted her teeth. First Mary wanted to visit with Mom. Then she wanted to hold Hannah. Now she wanted Grandpa to show her around the greenhouse. Who had Mary come to visit, anyway?

For the next half hour, Mary followed Grandpa around the greenhouse, asking questions and exclaiming how exciting it must be to work there.

Rachel stood to one side, nibbling on a fingernail and trying to be patient. At this rate, she and Mary would never have any fun together. The big day had turned into a disappointing day!

Chapter 7
Wishful Thinking

"Let's go look for Cuddles and Snowball now," Rachel said after Grandpa had shown Mary every part of the greenhouse.

"Where do you think they might be?" Mary asked.

Rachel shrugged. "Knowing Cuddles, they could be almost anywhere."

"I thought about bringing Stripes," Mary said. "But Mom thought he'd be too much trouble. Besides, now that Cuddles has a kitten of her own, she probably would have ignored my cat."

"Why do you think that?" Rachel asked.

"Cuddles has her kitten to play with now."

Rachel shook her head. "Cuddles usually hides from Snowball, because that lively little kitten can be a real pescht!"

"Does Cuddles ever get jealous when you give Snowball too much attention?" Mary asked as they headed for the creek.

Rachel nodded. "I think she does sometimes, and I can't blame her. I was jealous of Hannah when she was first born and got so much attention. That's one reason I went to Hershey Park with Sherry and her brother and didn't get Mom and Pap's permission."

Mary's eyebrows shot up. "You went to Hershey Park without asking your folks?"

"Jah."

As they walked along the path, Rachel told Mary how she'd gone to Hershey Park with her English friend Sherry and her brother, Dave. "When I wandered off and couldn't find them, I got really scared." Rachel shivered as she remembered the fear she'd felt that day. "I didn't know if I'd ever see any of my family again."

"How did you get home?" Mary asked.

"Sherry and Dave found me in the parking lot." Rachel swallowed hard, remembering how glad she'd felt when they'd gotten home.

"I'll bet your folks were really upset because you ran off without telling them," Mary said.

Rachel nodded. "I wasn't allowed to go anywhere except church for several weeks because of what I did."

Mary squeezed Rachel's hand. "If you ever visit me in Indiana, maybe we can go to the Fun Spot Amusement Park."

"That sounds great." Rachel felt good to know that

Mary wanted her to come for a visit. Maybe things were okay between the two of them after all. Maybe Mary wanted to be with Rachel as much as Rachel wanted to be with her.

"I don't see any sign of the cats here," Mary said as they approached the creek. "But since it's such a hot day, why don't we go wading so we can get cooled off?"

"That's a good idea!" Rachel flopped onto the grass, yanked off her sneakers, and plodded into the creek. Mary did the same.

Rachel tromped around, going from one side of the creek to the other, kicking water in all directions. "This is so much fun! The chilly *wasser* [water] feels good on my legs!"

"It felt good at first, but now I'm getting cold." Mary shivered, stepped onto the grass, and sank to her knees. "Brr. . ."

Playing in the creek alone wasn't nearly as much fun as it had been with Mary, so Rachel waded out of the water and took a seat on the grass.

Just then, she spotted Cuddles and Snowball leaping through the tall grass, batting at grasshoppers.

"There's my silly *katze* [cats]!" Rachel laughed and pointed at the cats. "Looks like they're having a good time!"

Mary jumped to her feet. "Let's see if we catch 'em!"

Rachel joined the chase. "Here, kitty, kitty!" she

called, clapping her hands.

Cuddles and Snowball acted as if they didn't want to be caught, for they scampered up the nearest tree and climbed all the way to the top.

Rachel groaned. "At this rate we'll never get to play with my cats."

"Let's go back to the house and see if Hannah's awake," Mary suggested.

Rachel shook her head. "It's too hot to be inside. Besides, the boppli usually sleeps most of the morning. I don't think she'll be awake yet."

Mary frowned. "Guess we'll have to find something else to do."

"Would you like to blow some bubbles?" Rachel asked.

Mary shook her head.

"Why don't we jump on the trampoline? That's always fun!"

"It's too hot."

"We could sit on the fence by the pasture and watch the horses."

"I don't think so."

Rachel sighed. "What would you like to do?"

Mary shrugged.

"We could go up to the house and sit on the porch swing," Rachel suggested.

"I guess that would be all right," Mary said.

The girls picked up their sneakers and started for the house. They were halfway there when the dinner bell rang. *Ding! Ding! Ding!*

"It must be time for lunch," Rachel said.

"I wonder why your mamm didn't call us to help her fix it," Mary said.

"She probably thought we wanted to play." Rachel sighed. "I know I did."

Mary hurried toward the house.

"Tell Mom I'll be in soon," Rachel called. "I'm going to the phone shed to make a couple of calls."

Mary gave a nod and kept walking.

If Orlie and Audra can come over after lunch, maybe Mary will feel more like playing, Rachel thought as she headed to the shed. *Besides, I did promise they could see her.*

"It's good to have you visiting with us," Pap said to Mary as everyone gathered around the table. "I'm sorry I wasn't here when you arrived, but the boys and I had a lot of work to do in the fields."

Mary smiled. "That's okay; I understand."

"Maybe we can make some homemade ice cream while you're here," Pap said.

Mary smacked her lips. "That sounds real good."

"I called and left a message on Audra's and Orlie's answering machines," Rachel spoke up. "I told them. . ."

Mom put her finger to her lips and looked at Rachel

over the top of her glasses. "Shh. . . It's time for prayer."

Rachel bowed her head with the others. *Dear God,* she silently prayed, *Thank You for this food. Thank You for bringing Mary here to visit. Help Audra and Orlie to hear my message and come to play. Help us to have lots of fun today. Amen.*

Rachel finished her prayer and opened her eyes. She was relieved to see that everyone else's eyes were open, too. Sometimes she prayed too fast and opened her eyes before the rest of the family did. Then she had to close them again and think of something else to pray about.

"Here you go." Mom handed Rachel a bowl of pickled beets.

Rachel forked several beets onto her plate and drew in a deep breath. "Yum." She loved the smell of pickled beets. She loved the way they tasted, too.

"As I was about to say before we had prayer. . . I went out to the phone shed before I came inside, and—"

"Say, Mary, I've been wondering about something," Jacob cut in.

"What's that?" Mary asked as she reached for a piece of ham.

"Do they have lightning bugs in Indiana?"

"The correct word is *fireflies*," Henry said before Mary could answer Jacob's question.

"Fireflies. . . Lightning bugs. . . They're both the same." Jacob turned to Mary and grinned. "Do they have any *lightning bugs* in Indiana?"

Mary nodded. "Some things are the same in Indiana as they are here, but some things are different."

"Like what?" Henry wanted to know.

"For one thing, Indiana doesn't have a lot of hills like Pennsylvania does."

Rachel nudged Mary's arm. "As I was saying before. . ."

Jacob pushed the salad bowl toward Mary. "What about stinkbugs? Do they have stinkbugs in Indiana?"

She nodded and crinkled her nose. "I don't like stinkbugs at all! They smell really bad—especially if they get squished!"

Grandpa chuckled. "I remember once when I was a boy, my brother Sam put a stinkbug in my bed." He slowly shook his head. "I rolled over on it, of course. Boy, did that critter ever smell up my bed. Phew!"

Everyone at the table laughed. Everyone but Rachel. She ground her teeth and clutched her fork so tightly that her fingers began to ache. She wished everyone would quit interrupting her and let her speak what was on her mind!

"One time, when I was a young girl, some boys at school put stinkbugs on the teacher's seat when she wasn't looking." Mom's nose twitched as she pushed her glasses back in place. "When the teacher sat down, the whole room smelled so horrible that we all had to hold our breath!"

"I think most everyone has a stinkbug story to tell," Pap said with a grin.

Rachel cleared her throat loudly. "Changing the subject. . . Before I came in for lunch, I went out to the phone shed and called—"

Jacob bumped Rachel's foot under the table. "Remember the time we were having a picnic at the pond and a stinkbug landed on your piece of chicken?" He snorted. "I saved the day by squashing that stinky critter before you could eat it."

"I wasn't gonna eat the stinkbug!" Rachel frowned at Jacob. "And I wish you'd stop talking so I can say something!"

Mom shook her finger at Rachel. "How many times must I tell you not to use your outside voice when you're in the house?"

"Sorry, Mom," Rachel mumbled, "but I've been trying to say something ever since we sat down at the table. Every time I start to say it, someone cuts me off."

Mom patted Rachel's arm. "Just calm down, and say what's on your mind."

"I left messages for Audra and Orlie on their folks' answering machines. I invited them to come play this afternoon." Rachel turned to Mary and said, "I can't wait for you to meet Audra, and I know Orlie would like to see you again."

Mary nodded. "I'd like to see them, too."

"Waaa! Waaa!"

"It sounds like the boppli's awake," Mom said. "I'd better get her before she becomes too worked up."

"Would you like me to get Hannah for you, Aunt Miriam?" Mary asked eagerly. "I'd like to hold her again."

Mom smiled. "I appreciate the offer, but Hannah probably needs her windel changed. I'll also need to feed her."

Mary frowned as she stared at her plate. "Oh, all right."

"You can hold the boppli after lunch. By then she'll have been diapered and fed, so you won't have to worry about a thing," Mom said, rising from her chair.

A huge smile spread across Mary's face. "Okay!"

Rachel frowned. Once Mary got her hands on Hannah, she probably wouldn't want to play at all. She'd probably want to spend the rest of the day fussing over the baby.

After the lunch dishes were done, Mary asked Mom if she could hold Hannah.

"Of course you can." Mom smiled. "If you'd like to go into the living room and sit in the rocking chair, I'll get Hannah from her crib and bring her in to you."

Mary gave a quick nod.

"I thought we were going outside to play," Rachel

called as Mary started for the living room.

"We can play later, when Hannah's taking her afternoon nap." Mary scurried out of the kitchen.

Rachel groaned and slouched in her chair.

"Now don't look so gloomy," Mom said. "You and Mary can take turns holding the boppli."

"I don't want to hold the boppli. I want to go outside and play!"

Mom squinted at Rachel. "Mary's your guest. You should be willing to do what she wants while she's here, don't you think?"

Rachel turned the palms of her hands upward. "Guess I may as well since there's no sign of Orlie or Audra."

"Maybe they didn't get your message. They could be gone for the day, you know." Mom patted Rachel's arm. "I'm going to get Hannah. Are you coming?"

"Jah, okay," Rachel mumbled.

When Mom had given Hannah to Mary, she left to get some canning jars out of the basement.

Rachel sat on the sofa and picked at some lint on the throw pillow beside her. Sitting in the stuffy living room was just plain boring! Watching Mary fuss over the baby was enough to make her feel sick.

"It's sure hot in here. Aren't you hot, Mary?" Rachel questioned.

Mary shook her head. "I feel just fine."

"Sitting here is boring. Aren't you bored?"

Mary stroked the top of Hannah's head. "Who could be bored when they're holding such a bundle of sweetness?"

Rachel tapped her foot against the hardwood floor. *Thump! Thump! Thump!* She wished Orlie and Audra were here. She wished Mary wasn't so interested in holding the baby.

"It would sure be nice if I had a baby sister." Mary leaned over and kissed Hannah's cheek. "She's so soft and cuddly."

"My bussli is soft and cuddly, too," Rachel said.

"That may be true, but a kitten's not nearly as soft and cuddly as a human baby."

Tap! Tap! Tap!

Rachel jumped up. "Someone's knocking on the back door. I'll be right back!" She raced out of the room. When she opened the back door, she was pleased to see Orlie.

"I got your message," he said with a crooked grin. "So I came to play." He looked past Rachel, into the kitchen. "Where's your cousin?"

Rachel motioned to the living room door. "Mary's in there, holding my baby sister."

"Is she comin' out to play?"

"I don't know, but I'll ask." Rachel raced back to the living room and screeched to a stop in front of Mary's chair. "Orlie's here! He came over to play and wants us to come outside."

"You go ahead," said Mary. "I'm busy holding Hannah."

"Just take the boppli to Mom and Pap's room and put her back in the crib. She'll be fine."

Mary shook her head. "I don't want to go outside right now. I want to stay in here and hold the boppli."

Rachel frowned. "You've held her long enough. Let's go outside and play."

"I'd rather not."

"Fine then, suit yourself! I'm going outside where it's cooler!" Rachel stomped across the room and raced out the back door, banging it behind her. She found Orlie sitting on the porch step, holding Snowball.

Rachel flopped down beside him. "Where'd you find my kitten?"

"She wandered into the yard with Cuddles." Orlie stroked the kitten's head. "Cuddles took off for the barn, but Snowball ran onto the porch and leaped into my arms."

Rachel grunted. "She wouldn't come when I called her earlier. She and Cuddles ran up a tree out by the creek."

Orlie looked at Rachel and squinted his eyes. "Is something wrong? You seem kind of cranky."

"I'm not cranky. I'm just— Oh, never mind." Rachel jumped up. "Are we going to play or not?"

"Just the two of us?"

Rachel nodded. "Jacob's in the fields helping Pap and Henry, so he can't play at all today. I invited Audra over, but she must not have gotten my message yet."

"What about Mary? Isn't she coming out to play?"

Rachel shook her head. "She's still holding Hannah and doesn't want to play!"

"I guess it's just the two of us then." Orlie placed the kitten on the ground and ran into the yard. He sat on the grass and moved his arms in a rowing motion.

"What do you think you're doing?" Rachel asked. She had seen Orlie do some pretty odd things, but this seemed weirder than usual.

"I'm pretending that I'm rowing a boat. Come on, Rachel. Sit down and pretend you're rowing a boat, too."

"I don't want to."

"Aw, come on, Rachel. It's much cooler down here, and if you pretend really hard, you'll think you're sailing across the water in a real boat."

Rachel rolled her eyes. "You're so weird, Orlie."

"Am not. I'm just good at imagining and wishing for things."

"You wish you were in a boat?"

"Jah, I sure do."

"Well, I wish Mary would come outside. And I wish the three of us were jumping on the trampoline," Rachel muttered.

Orlie stopped rowing. "Does your cousin think she's too good to play with me? Is that why she's staying in the house?"

Rachel shook her head. "I don't think Mary thinks she's too good to play with you. She just wants to—"

"Maybe Mary's turned into a snob since she moved away."

"My cousin's not a snob!" Rachel's face heated up. "I think you're jumping to conclusions!"

"People change," Orlie said. "Maybe living in Indiana has changed Mary."

Rachel shook her head so hard that the ribbons on her kapp flipped around her face. "That's *lecherich* [ridiculous]! Mary's the same girl she was when she lived here in Pennsylvania!"

Even as the words slipped off Rachel's tongue, she wondered if they were true. Ever since Mary had arrived, she'd been acting differently than she had before she moved.

Rachel flopped onto the grass. What if Mary really *had* changed? What if they weren't close friends anymore? Maybe things would never be the same between her and Mary. Maybe all the fun Rachel had thought she and Mary would have had just been wishful thinking.

Chapter 8
Nosing Around

Mary had been at Rachel's house for three whole days before Audra finally showed up after breakfast one morning.

"My family and I went to Illinois for my cousin's wedding," Audra told Rachel. "We got back last night, and when my daed checked the messages in the phone shed, he said one was from you."

Rachel nodded. "I wanted you to meet my cousin Mary. She got here three days ago."

Audra smiled. "I would like to meet her. Where is she?"

"In the kitchen, writing a letter to her mamm." Rachel opened the door wider. "Come in, and I'll introduce you."

Audra glanced at the barn. "Brian came with me. He saw Jacob when we got here, and they went out to the barn."

"That's good. Maybe they won't bother us girls while we play."

When they entered the kitchen, Rachel motioned to Mary, who sat at the table, writing a letter.

"This is my cousin Mary," Rachel said to Audra.

Mary looked up and smiled.

"And this is my friend Audra Burkholder." Rachel patted Audra's back.

"It's nice to meet you, Audra," Mary said. "Rachel's told me a lot about you in her letters."

Audra smiled shyly. "She told me about you, too."

"Audra came over to play," Rachel said. "You're gonna join us, aren't you?"

Mary nodded. "I just finished my letter, so as soon as I put it in the mailbox, I'll be ready to play."

"The mailman's already come by our place," Rachel said. "So you may as well wait until tomorrow morning to put the letter in the box."

"Okay. Let's go outside then," Mary said.

Rachel smiled. At least her cousin was willing to play today. Of course, that could be because Mom had taken Hannah to the doctor for a checkup, and they weren't back yet. Rachel figured if Hannah were here, Mary would probably be holding her right now and wouldn't want to play at all.

"What should we do first?" Audra asked as the girls headed outside.

"We could play in the barn," Mary suggested.

Rachel shook her head. "I'd rather not. Jacob's there

with Brian. Knowing my teasing bruder, he'd probably find something mean to do if we went out there."

"My bruder would, too," Audra said. "I think he looks for ways to tease me."

Rachel sat on the porch step. Mary and Audra sat on either side of her.

"How's Brian's problem?" Rachel asked, looking at Audra. "Is he doing any better?"

"Not really." Audra wrinkled her nose. "He had an accident while we were at Grandma and Grandpa's."

"What kind of accident?" Mary wanted to know. "Did he fall and hurt himself?"

Audra shook her head. "Sometimes Brian wets the bed."

Mary gasped. "I thought only bopplin wet the bed!"

Rachel clenched her fingers, remembering how Mom had told her that she used to wet the bed. Rachel was glad she couldn't remember that. She hoped no one else in the family remembered it, either. She decided she needed to quickly change the subject.

"Is anyone thirsty?" she asked.

Mary nodded.

Audra shrugged.

"I think I'll go inside and get us something cold to drink," Rachel said.

"That sounds good." Mary smiled. "Do you need my help?"

"Thanks, but I can manage." Rachel jumped up and

scurried into the house.

When she opened the refrigerator, she found a jug of Pap's homemade root beer on the top shelf. She lifted it out, grabbed three paper cups from the pantry, and headed for the door.

Rachel was about to step onto the porch when she heard her name mentioned.

"Jah, that's right," said Mary, "Rachel is. . ."

Whoosh! Snowball leaped onto the porch and darted between Rachel's legs, nearly knocking her off her feet.

Rachel righted herself in time, but the jug of root beer slipped out of her hand and fell to the porch with a splat!

"Ach no!" Rachel cried. Cold, sticky root beer covered her dress, legs, and the porch floor.

Mary jumped up. "What happened, Rachel?"

"I was standing in the doorway, and Snowball ran between my legs." Rachel frowned. "She knocked me off balance, and I dropped the jug of root beer."

Audra pointed to Rachel's dress and laughed. "Looks like you had a root beer bath!"

"It's not funny." Rachel slowly shook her head. "Now I have to go inside and change my dress."

"While you're doing that, I'll get the mop and clean the mess off the porch," Mary said.

"Okay, thanks." Rachel scurried into the house, mumbling, "Always trouble somewhere!"

When Rachel returned to the porch wearing a clean

dress, she was pleased to see that the root beer had been cleaned off the floor and a carton of milk was on the small table near the door. Mary and Audra sat in the porch swing, talking with their heads together.

When Rachel approached the swing, they stopped talking.

She frowned and squinted at them. "Were you two saying something bad about me?"

"Of course not," Mary said, shaking her head.

"Then why did you stop talking when I came out?"

Audra shrugged.

Mary stared at the floor.

"You *were* saying something bad about me." Rachel folded her arms and frowned. "I know you were."

"You're jumping to conclusions," Mary said. "Audra and I were just talking about the painted rocks you made for us."

"That's right," Audra agreed. "We think you have lots of talent."

Rachel smiled. "Really?"

Both girls nodded.

"I wish I could paint the way you do," Mary said.

Rachel squeezed in between them on the swing. "Everyone has something they're good at. I just happen to be good at painting on rocks."

"My mamm says I'm good at sewing, and if I keep practicing, someday I'll be as good as she is." Audra looked over at Mary. "What are you good at?"

Mary thumped her chin a couple of times. "Let's see now. . ."

"You're good at baking cookies. The ones you helped Mom bake last night were *appeditlich* [delicious]."

Mary smiled. "They were pretty good. Should we have some now?"

"Maybe later." Rachel jumped up. "Let's jump on the trampoline for a while!"

Audra clapped her hands and jumped up, too. "Oh, good; I love jumping on your trampoline!"

The girls ran down the steps, hurried across the yard, and climbed onto the trampoline. They'd only been jumping a few minutes when Jacob and Brian rushed out of the barn and raced over to the trampoline.

"Oh no," Rachel groaned. "Looks like we've got company."

"Should we get off?" Mary asked.

"No way!" Rachel shook her head. "We were here first, so we're staying!"

"Let's have some fun!" Jacob hollered as he and Brian climbed onto the trampoline.

Boing! Boing! Boing! Jacob jumped so high that all three girls toppled over.

Jacob laughed.

Brian laughed.

Rachel glared at Jacob.

Audra glared at Brian.

Mary climbed off the trampoline. "I think I'll watch from here," she said.

Brian did a few jumps; then he flipped into the air. "Woo-hoo! This is so much fun!" He bounced high again, causing Rachel to flip into the air and fall onto the ground.

"Oomph!" She brushed some chunks of grass from her dress; then she scrambled to her feet and shook her finger at Brian. "You'd better be careful jumping like that or you might wet your pants!"

Brian's face turned red as a ripe tomato. He scowled at Audra. "Did you tell Rachel about my problem?"

"What problem is that?" Jacob asked before Audra could respond.

"He wets the bed," Rachel blurted out.

Jacob nudged Brian's arm. "Is that true?"

Brian hung his head, and his face turned even redder. "I'm gonna get even with you for this, Audra," he muttered. "I can't believe you'd blab something like that to Rachel."

"I–I'm sorry," Audra sputtered. "I didn't think she would tell anyone."

Tears stung Rachel's eyes. "I—I didn't meant to say what I did. My tongue just slipped."

Brian looked over at Jacob with a pathetic expression. "I don't wet the bed all the time, but when I do it's so embarrassing. Mom says I'll grow out of it someday, and I sure hope it's soon."

Jacob thumped Brian on the back a couple of times. "It's okay. I won't tell anyone; I promise." He looked at Rachel and frowned. "You'd better keep your nose out of other people's business, and you'd better keep quiet about Brian's problem. If you don't, I'll tell everyone that you used to wet the bed."

"I—I only did it until I was five." A tear slipped out of Rachel's eye and rolled down her cheek. "You can ask Mom if you don't believe me."

"Even so, if you tell anyone else about Brian's problem, then I'll tell them about yours," Jacob said.

"I won't say a word," Rachel promised. Even though her bed-wetting days were in the past, she didn't want anyone else to know.

"I think we should change the subject," Mary said.

"You're right." Audra climbed off the trampoline. "I think we girls should go up to Rachel's room and play with her dolls."

Rachel didn't play with dolls anymore. She felt too grown-up for that. Still, it would be better than staying out here with the boys.

"All right," she said with a nod. "The boys can have the trampoline all to themselves!"

Later that day, when Mom got home, Mary asked if she

could hold Hannah again.

"Jah, sure," Mom said. "You can hold her until I'm ready to start lunch." She looked at Rachel and smiled. "Did you and Mary have a good morning?"

Rachel nodded. "Audra and Brian came over to play, but they went home awhile ago." She hoped Mary wouldn't mention what had been said about Brian wetting the bed. Rachel didn't want a lecture from Mom for blabbing something she shouldn't have blabbed.

"I'm glad Mary was able to meet Audra." Mom smiled at Mary. "Did you enjoy spending time with Rachel's new friend?"

Mary nodded. "We jumped on the trampoline for a while, and then we played with Rachel's dolls." She sat in the living room rocker. "I'm ready to hold Hannah now."

Mom placed the baby in Mary's lap. "I'm going to the kitchen to get lunch started. I'll call you when it's time to set the table," she said, looking at Rachel.

Rachel nodded.

When Mom left the room, Rachel sighed with relief. She was thankful Mary hadn't said anything about Brian wetting the bed.

"Since you're busy holding Hannah, I think I'll go out to the barn and see if Cuddles or Snowball is there," Rachel said to Mary.

"Sure, go ahead." Mary hummed as she rocked the baby.

Rachel rolled her eyes and hurried from the room. She didn't know why Mary thought she had to hold Hannah so much.

As soon as Rachel opened the barn door, she heard voices. It sounded like Pap and Henry were in one of the horse's stalls.

"When are Grandpa and Grandma Yoder leaving?" she heard Henry ask.

"Within the next week or so," Pap said.

Rachel held her breath and leaned against the wall as she continued to listen to their conversation.

Henry said something else, but Rachel couldn't make out the words. She inched a bit closer to the horses' stalls.

"Wisconsin's a nice place. I think they'll. . ." Pap's voice trailed off.

Rats! Rachel thought. *I wish I knew what else he said. Are Grandpa and Grandma Yoder moving to Wisconsin? Oh, I sure hope not!*

She moved a bit closer to the stall, and—*ploop!*— stepped right in a bucket.

"Oh no!" Rachel groaned as she lifted her bare foot out of the bucket. It was covered with white paint!

"Rachel, is that you?" Pap stuck his head around the corner of the stall. He looked at Rachel, and his mouth dropped open. "What are you doing with your foot in that bucket of paint?"

"I—I didn't do it on purpose," Rachel stammered. "I was trying to hear what you and Henry were saying, and—"

"You were listening in on our conversation?"

She nodded. "I heard you say something about Grandpa and Grandpa Yoder moving to Wisconsin, and—"

"Grandpa and Grandma aren't moving anywhere," Henry said, stepping out of the stall. "They're going to Wisconsin on a trip, that's all."

Rachel's face heated up. "Oh. I—I guess I must have jumped to conclusions."

"Well, you'd better jump out of that paint bucket and wash off your foot," Pap said. "And no more listening to other people's conversations!"

Rachel hopped on one foot out the barn door and over to the hose. Then she turned on the water and washed the paint off her foot. "Trouble, trouble, trouble," she mumbled and grumbled.

When Rachel was sure she had all the paint washed off, she hurried back to the house, no longer in the mood to play with the cats.

She found Mom in the kitchen, making ham and cheese sandwiches. "Your timing is perfect, Rachel," she said. "I was just about to call you."

"Do you want me to set the table?" Rachel asked.

"Jah, and then I'd like you to go down to the greenhouse and tell your *grossdaadi* [grandfather] that lunch is about ready."

"Okay."

Rachel hurried and set the table; then she raced out the back door and headed for Grandpa's greenhouse. She was halfway there when she spotted Grandpa coming out of the greenhouse with Abe Byler, a member of the school board. The two men stood with their backs to Rachel.

I wonder what they're talking about, Rachel thought. *If I move closer I might be able to hear what they're saying.* She ducked under the branches of the maple tree near the greenhouse and leaned against the trunk of the tree.

"Jah, that's right," Abe said to Grandpa. "Why, it's my understanding that the whole school system seems to be falling to ruins."

"That's too bad." Grandpa slowly shook his head. "It's a real shame."

"And that teacher is so lazy. I think she ought to be fired from her job." Abe grunted. "Do you know that. . ."

Bzzz. . . Bzzz. . . Bzzz. . .

Rachel swatted at a bee buzzing around her head. She had to hear the rest of what Abe had to say. This was all so shocking! She'd never thought her teacher, Elizabeth, was lazy!

Maybe I should say something, she thought. *Abe and*

Grandpa need to know that Elizabeth's not lazy. She's a wonderful teacher. Oh, I hope she won't lose her job!

Rachel was about to move away from the tree, when—*Bzzz. . . Bzzz.* That pesky old bee stung her right on the nose!

"Yeow!" Rachel waved her hands and jumped up and down.

Grandpa whirled around. "What's the matter with you, Rachel? Why are you carrying on like that?"

"A big old *iem* [bee] stung me right here." Rachel pointed to her nose and tried not to cry.

"I'm sorry that happened. Where were you standing when the iem got you?" Grandpa asked. "There might be a nest someplace that needs to be removed."

Rachel motioned to the tree. "I was right there."

"Just what were you doing under the tree?" Grandpa's eyes narrowed. "Were you listening to Abe's and my conversation?"

Rachel nodded slowly as tears clouded her vision. She reached under her glasses and wiped them away. "I—I heard Abe say that our whole school is in ruins, and that—" *Sniff! Sniff!* "That Elizabeth is lazy and should be fired."

Deep wrinkles formed across Abe's forehead. "I never said that."

"Jah, you did. I heard you say it." Rachel sniffed a couple more times. "Elizabeth's not lazy. She works real hard. She's the best teacher anyone could ever want."

Abe looked at Grandpa then back at Rachel. "For your information, I was talking about another school district—the one where my brother lives. It's his granddaughter's schoolteacher who's gotten lazy, not yours."

"Oh, I'm so glad." Rachel covered her mouth with the palm of her hand. "I—I didn't mean that I'm glad your granddaughter's schoolteacher is lazy. I just meant to say—"

"I know what you meant." Abe looked back at Grandpa. "Guess this is my fault for spreading a bit of gossip. I really shouldn't have said anything about this at all. I hope you won't repeat anything I told you."

Grandpa shook his head. "Of course not."

Abe turned toward his buggy. "I should be on my way now." He gave Rachel a sympathetic look. "I hope that the iem *schteche* [sting] doesn't hurt too much."

She forced a smile and shook her head. "Guess I deserve it for nosing around."

Grandpa and Abe both nodded their heads.

Abe climbed into his buggy and drove away. Rachel stepped up to Grandpa and said, "Mom sent me to tell you that lunch is about ready."

"All right, but let me look at that *naas* [nose] of yours first. Then we'll head up to the house." Grandpa bent down and studied Rachel's nose. "I can see where that pesky iem got you all right. Your naas is a bit swollen."

Rachel touched her nose and winced. "It stings like crazy, too."

"It'll feel better once your mamm makes a paste with a little water and some baking soda. She'll slather that on your naas, and it should draw the stinger right out."

"I—I hope so."

As they walked toward the house, Grandpa rested his hand on Rachel's shoulder. "Proverbs 11:13 tells us: 'A gossip betrays a confidence, but a trustworthy man keeps a secret.' You've become a bit of a *schnuppich* [snoopy] gossip lately. I hope you've learned a lesson today about the problem that could come from listening in on someone's conversation."

Rachel nodded. "No more nosing around for me!"

Chapter 9
Babysitting

Rachel, Mary, and Mom were in the kitchen getting things ready for the bonfire they'd be having later. Tonight was Mary's last night with Rachel and her family, so Pap had said they could do something special. Rachel had asked for the bonfire, and Mary said she wanted to roast hot dogs and marshmallows. Rachel's sister, Esther, and her husband, Rudy, would be joining them, too.

Rachel had just removed a jar of mustard from the refrigerator when she heard buggy wheels rumble up the driveway. "That must be Esther and Rudy," she said to Mary, who stood near the sink, cutting dill pickles into thick slices.

"It's Aunt Karen, Uncle Amos, and Gerald," Mom said, peering out the kitchen window. "Grandpa and Grandpa Yoder are with them, too."

"Do they know Mary's leaving tomorrow?" Rachel asked.

"Jah, I'm sure they do."

"Did they come to say good-bye to Mary?"

"I'm sure they'll say good-bye. They've also come to drop off Gerald, because they'll be leaving early in the morning."

Rachel's forehead wrinkled. "Leaving for where?"

"Gerald's mamm and daed are going to Wisconsin with Grandpa and Grandma Yoder to attend Aunt Karen's sister's wedding." Mom started for the door. "I'm sure you knew that, Rachel."

"Guess I must have forgot," Rachel mumbled.

"Why aren't they taking Gerald to the wedding?" Mary wanted to know.

Mom glanced over her shoulder and smiled. "Gerald gets fussy when he rides in a car. Aunt Karen and Uncle Amos think Gerald will be happier staying here with us."

"Oh, great!" Rachel sank into a chair at the table. Gerald could be a real handful at times. He always pestered Rachel with a bunch of questions and expected her to give him horsey rides. "How long does Gerald have to stay with us?" she asked.

"Just for a week." Mom opened the back door and stepped onto the porch. Rachel and Mary followed.

When Grandpa and Grandma Yoder came up the walk, Mary ran out to greet them.

"We hear you're leaving tomorrow," Grandpa said, patting Mary's head.

Mary nodded slowly. Rachel wondered if her cousin might be on the verge of tears.

Grandma bent down and hugged Mary. "When you get home, tell your folks we said hello and that we'll try to come to Indiana for a visit soon."

Mary smiled. "That would be real nice."

"If you make a trip to Indiana, maybe I can go with you," Rachel was quick to say.

Grandpa Yoder nodded, and Grandma Yoder gently squeezed Rachel's shoulder.

"Can you all stay and have supper with us?" Mom asked Uncle Amos, since he'd been the one driving the horse and buggy.

He shook his head. "I'm afraid not. Our driver will pick us up early tomorrow morning. We really need to go home, finish packing our suitcases, and get to bed early." He set Gerald's small suitcase on the porch and scooped the little boy into his arms. "Be good for Uncle Levi and Aunt Miriam," he said.

Tears welled in Gerald's eyes, and his chin quivered like a leaf on a windy day. Pretty soon the tears started to flow, and then Gerald's nose began to run.

Aunt Karen wiped Gerald's nose with a tissue; then she patted his back. "You'll have a good time here with Rachel. The two of you can do many fun things together."

Rachel cringed. Did Aunt Karen think she wanted

Gerald hanging around her the whole time he was here? She hoped Gerald didn't think that, because she had better things to do than babysit her gabby little cousin for a whole week!

Mom nudged Rachel's arm and motioned to Gerald's suitcase. "Would you please take that up to Jacob's room? That's where Gerald will sleep while he's here."

"Jah, okay." Rachel picked up Gerald's suitcase and went into the house. At least Gerald would sleep in Jacob's room and not hers. That meant Rachel would have a few hours to herself, even if it was only when she was asleep.

When Rachel came back downstairs, she spotted Gerald sitting tearfully in the middle of the living room floor, with Mary kneeling by his side.

"His folks just left, and he's feeling sad," Mary said, looking up at Rachel.

"Let's take him out to the barn to play with my kitten," Rachel suggested. "That should help take his mind off his troubles."

"That's a good idea." Mary took Gerald's hand and helped him to his feet. "*Kumme* [come], let's go play with the bussli."

"Bussli," Gerald said, slightly smiling. Rachel hoped that meant he would not cry any more today.

"We'd better check with my mamm first," Rachel said. "Just in case she needs us for something."

The three of them hurried to the kitchen. They found Mom making a pitcher of lemonade.

"Do we have time to take Gerald to the barn to play with Snowball?" Rachel asked.

Mom nodded and smiled. "Esther and Rudy won't be here for another hour or so. Since everything is almost ready for our bonfire, I think there's enough time for you to play in the barn."

"Okay. Ring the dinner bell when Esther and Rudy arrive, please," Rachel said as she, Mary, and Gerald headed out the door.

When they entered the barn, they found Snowball sleeping on a bale of hay, but they saw no sign of Cuddles. Rachel figured it was for the best. Cuddles had seemed irritable lately—probably because Snowball pestered her all the time. She might not take too kindly to a rowdy little boy bothering her, too.

"Bussli! Bussli!" Gerald squealed as he lunged for the kitten.

Yeow! Snowball leaped into the air, darted across the barn floor, and scurried up the ladder to the hayloft. She obviously didn't care for rowdy little boys, either.

Gerald scrunched up his nose, and his face turned crimson as he stomped his feet. "Kumme, bussli. Kumme!"

"I don't think the kitten wants to play right now," Rachel said. "Maybe we should find something else to do."

"Waaa! Waaa!" Tears streamed down Gerald's face as he shook his head. "Bussli!"

Rachel covered her ears. *"Ich kann sell net geh* [I cannot tolerate that]*!* You can't play with the bussli right now, so you need to stop crying!"

"Waaa! Waaa!"

"You don't have to yell at him, Rachel," Mary said. "It's only making things worse."

Rachel shrugged. "Have you got any idea how to make him stop crying?"

"Why don't we blow some bubbles?" Mary suggested. She leaned over and put her face close to Gerald's. "Would you like to blow some bubbles, Gerald?"

Gerald stopped crying as quickly as he'd started. "Jah," he said, nodding his head. *"Blos* [bubble]*!"*

Rachel pointed to a plastic jug across the room. "I think there's a batch of bubble solution on the shelf over there." She hurried off and returned with a jar of bubble solution and three metal wands.

Mary made a couple of double bubbles. Rachel made a caterpillar by blowing several bubbles, the way Grandpa had shown her some time ago. Gerald made a few little bubbles, but mostly he just giggled and chased the bubbles Rachel and Mary made. At least he wasn't crying anymore. He hadn't asked for a horsey ride, either.

Ding! Ding! Ding!

Rachel jumped off the bale of hay she'd been sitting on. "There's the dinner bell! Esther and Rudy must be here, so we'd better go." She grabbed the bottle of bubble solution and put it back on the shelf.

"Blos! Blos!" Gerald hollered.

"We can make more bubbles another day," Rachel said. "Right now it's time to roast hot dogs and marshmallows!"

Gerald looked up at her and tipped his head. "Marshmallows?"

"That's right; now we'd better go!"

Gerald raced out of the barn, giggling all the way.

Rachel turned to Mary and rolled her eyes. "One minute he's crying; the next minute he's laughing. I just can't figure that little boy out."

Mary snickered. "I guess you're gonna have to learn how to figure him out, since he'll be with you for a whole week."

Rachel nodded and reached for Mary's hand. "I wish you could stay and help me babysit him. You do better with little ones than I do."

Mary shrugged as she skipped out the door. "I'm sure you and Gerald will get along just fine."

As Rachel sat around the bonfire with her family that evening, her eyes darted from the glow of the burning embers to the glittering fireflies rising from the grass. It was a peaceful evening, and if she hadn't felt so sad about Mary leaving in the morning, she'd have been perfectly content.

Rachel thought back to the night before Mary moved to Indiana, and how Mary had come to spend the night with her. She'd been sad that night, too. Saying good-bye to Mary the next day had nearly broken Rachel's heart. It had taken Rachel several weeks to adjust to Mary being gone.

Of course, Rachel thought, *it will be a little easier saying good-bye to Mary tomorrow, because I've made some new friends since she moved away. I have Audra and Sherry as friends now, and Mary's made some new friends in Indiana.*

As Rachel listened to her family sing a song about the joy of having friends, she thought about the miracle of friendship. Rachel and Mary had both changed some since Mary had moved away. Mary's visit hadn't gone exactly the way Rachel had hoped it would.

Even so, Rachel still enjoyed being with Mary, and she hoped that she and her cousin would always be good friends. She looked forward to the day she could go to Indiana to see Mary's new home.

Rachel jumped when she felt a tug on her hand.

Gerald, who sat between Rachel and Mary, pointed to the sky and said, *"Schtann* [Stars]."

Rachel smiled. "Jah, Gerald. See how the night

sparkles because of the stars?"

Gerald pointed upward again. "*Munn* [Moon]. Papa made the munn."

"No, Gerald," Rachel said with a shake of her head. "God made the munn. God made everything."

"That's right," Mary agreed. "The Bible says that God made the sun, moon, stars, and every living thing."

Gerald's forehead wrinkled, and he puckered his lips. "Everything?"

Mary and Rachel nodded at the same time.

Gerald pointed to himself. "God made me?"

"That's right," said Rachel's sister Esther who sat in a chair on the other side of Rachel. She placed both hands against her bulging stomach and smiled. "He also knows my little one before it's even born."

"I wish I could be here when your boppli comes," Mary said with a sad expression. "I love bopplin. . .and little kinner, too." She looked over at Rachel and sighed. "You're lucky to be able to babysit Gerald for a whole week. I wish his folks would have brought him sooner so I could have helped entertain him."

Rachel grunted. "I'll send him home with you, if you like."

"I would like that," Mary said, "but I don't think Gerald's mamm and daed would be too happy if they came home from Wisconsin and discovered that he had gone home with me."

"No, I guess not." Rachel leaned closer to Mary and whispered, "I need to know something before you go."

"What's that?" Mary asked.

"Do you wish you hadn't come here for a visit?"

"No, of course not," Mary said with a shake of her head. "Why would you even ask me a question like that?"

Rachel moistened her lips with the tip of her tongue. "Sometimes it seemed like you'd rather be with Hannah than me."

"I'm sorry if it seemed that way. I really did enjoy being with you, but holding baby Hannah has been special for me, too." Mary reached for Rachel's hand and gently squeezed it. "You'll always be my good friend, and I'm really glad I came."

Rachel smiled and tilted her head back to look at the starry sky again. *Thank You, God, for making such a beautiful world.* She looked down at Gerald, who'd climbed into Grandpa's lap and fallen asleep; then she closed her eyes and finished her prayer. *Thank You, God, for everyone in my family. . .even Gerald.*

Chapter 10
Another Good-bye

As Rachel ran water into the sink to wash the breakfast dishes, she heard Mom and Pap talking in the hall. Her ears perked up when Pap mentioned her name. She knew she wasn't supposed to eavesdrop, but how could she not listen when they were talking about her?

She reached into the cupboard for the dishwashing soap while she strained to hear what Pap was saying.

"That's right, Miriam. I think Rachel needs to. . ." Pap's voice trailed off.

Rachel squirted the dishwashing liquid into the sink full of warm water. She heard the back door shut and figured Mom and Pap must have gone outside to finish their conversation. She was tempted to leave the dishes and follow them. She knew if she did, though, Mom would ask if she had finished washing the dishes.

Rachel dropped the sponge into the dishwater and frowned. There were no bubbles. Not even one. "Now that's sure strange."

She grabbed the bottle of dishwashing liquid, squirted it into the water again, and swished the sponge around in the water. Still no bubbles!

"What in all the world?" Rachel stared at the bottle. It wasn't dishwashing liquid at all! It was window cleaner! "Guess I should have read the label first," she muttered.

She pulled the plug on the drain to let the water out. Then she filled the sink with fresh water.

She set the bottle of window cleaner back in the cupboard and reached for another bottle. This time she carefully read the label to make sure it was dishwashing liquid. She squirted some of the liquid into the warm water and sloshed the sponge around. Several bubbles drifted to the ceiling.

"I wish I didn't have dishes to do," Rachel grumbled. "I wish I were upstairs helping Mary pack."

She swallowed around the lump in her throat. *I hope I'll get to visit Mary in Indiana sometime. It would be fun to see what life is like there. If school wasn't starting next week, I'd ask if I could go home with Mary now.*

Whoosh! The kitchen door flew open, and Gerald barreled in. "Blos!" he shouted, pointing to the colorful bubbles rising to the ceiling.

"Jah, Gerald, the bubbles are coming from my dishwater," Rachel said.

Gerald waved his hand in the air. "Blow blos?"

Rachel shook her head. "There's no time to blow bubbles right now. I need to finish washing the dishes."

Gerald's chin quivered, and his eyes filled with tears.

Rachel sighed. "Don't start crying," she said. "I have no patience for that this morning."

Just then Mary stepped into the room, carrying her suitcase. "I'm all packed and ready to go. I just have to wait for Carolyn to pick me up."

Rachel glanced at the clock on the opposite wall. "She should be here soon, I expect."

Mary nodded. "I'm anxious to see my family again, but I wish I could stay with you a while longer. Our visit seemed awfully short."

"Short!" Gerald hollered as he pointed to himself.

Rachel giggled. "I've heard Gerald's daed call him short, so Gerald must be mimicking him," she said to Mary.

Mary nodded. "Some little kinner like to do that."

Rachel heard the rumble of a vehicle in the driveway outside, followed by *Beep! Beep!*

"That must be Carolyn," Mary said. "I think it's time for us to say good-bye."

Rachel hugged Mary then followed her out the door. Gerald tagged along behind her. When they stepped onto the porch, Rachel saw Mom, Dad, and Grandpa talking to Carolyn by her van.

As Rachel, Mary, and Gerald headed that way, Jacob

and Henry came out of the barn. Soon everyone had gathered around Mary, hugging and saying their good-byes.

Just before Mary got into Carolyn's car, Rachel gave her one final hug. "Danki for coming," she said.

"You're welcome. See you soon, I hope." Mary climbed into the passenger's seat and shut the door.

As Carolyn's van drove away, Rachel watched until it was out of sight. Then she turned to Grandpa and said, "I need to keep busy so I don't miss Mary too much. Do you have some work you need me to do in the greenhouse this morning?"

He nodded and smiled. "Jah, sure. I'd be pleased to have your help, Rachel."

Rachel smiled as she headed for the greenhouse. During the time Mary had been visiting, she hadn't helped Grandpa at all. It would be good to water, trim, and repot some plants. It would be nice to see and smell the beauty of all those plants and flowers, too.

"Where ya goin'?"

Rachel stopped walking and turned around. Gerald looked up at her with an eager expression.

"I'm going to the greenhouse to help Grandpa."

"Okay." Gerald grabbed Rachel's hand. "Let's go!"

"No, Gerald. I'm going to the greenhouse to work." Rachel pointed to the house. "Why don't you go see if my mamm has something for you to do?"

Gerald hung tightly to Rachel's hand. "I go with you."

Rachel was tempted to argue but knew if she said no, Gerald would cry. Rachel just couldn't stand Gerald's crying!

"Okay, Gerald," she said with a sigh, "but you have to be good in the greenhouse and stay out of my way. Is that understood?"

Gerald nodded and looked up at her with a crooked grin.

When Rachel entered the greenhouse with Gerald, she was surprised to see Grandpa in one corner, standing on his head again.

"I'll be with you in a minute," Grandpa said as he peered at Rachel from his upside-down position. "I'm not done clearing my head, and I need to do this so I'll have a good start to my day."

Gerald raced across the room, flopped on the floor, and stood on his head beside Grandpa.

Rachel snickered. "Say, Grandpa, how come you stand on your head out here instead of in your bedroom?"

"I used to do that," he responded. "But since I got the greenhouse, I decided to do it out here among all these *wunderbaar* [wonderful] plants that give off oxygen."

"I've been in the greenhouse many times, and until a few weeks ago, I never saw you stand on your head," Rachel said.

Grandpa chuckled. "I always did it before you came out. I was afraid if you saw me like this you might laugh."

"I probably would have," Rachel admitted, "but I'm getting used to it now."

Ding! Ding! The bell on the greenhouse door rang, letting Rachel know a customer had come in.

Grandpa quickly dropped his feet to the floor.

Gerald did the same.

Rachel was surprised to see the man who had bought strawberries from her earlier this summer step into the greenhouse. After she'd put the basket of berries on the front seat of his car, she didn't think she would ever see him again.

"You know those strawberries I sat on earlier this summer?" he said, looking at Rachel.

She nodded slowly, wondering if he was going to scold her about that mishap again.

He smacked his lips and grinned. "My wife made strawberry jam from the smashed berries, and it turned out real good."

Rachel sighed with relief. "I'm glad to hear it. Was your wife able to get the berry juice out of your pants?"

"Oh yes. She soaked them in cold water and then

sprayed them with something that's good for stains." The man looked over at Grandpa, who'd taken a seat on a stool by the workbench where he repotted plants. "Today's my wife's birthday, so I came here to buy her a nice indoor plant."

Grandpa nodded at Rachel and said, "Would you like to show the man some plants?"

"Okay." Rachel led the way to the part of the greenhouse where the houseplants were kept. The man followed. So did Gerald.

Gerald reached up and touched the leaf of an ivy plant.

"No, Gerald," Rachel said. "Don't start fooling with things."

She moved down the row until she came to a shelf full of African violets. "Here's one with pretty pink blooms."

"That's a nice one. I really like it," the man said. "I think I'll take it."

Rachel started to reach for the plant when Gerald bumped her arm. The pot tipped over, spilling dirt all over the man's shirt!

Rachel shook her finger at Gerald. "I told you to stay out of the way! Now look what's happened!"

Tears welled in Gerald's eyes, and he tipped his head back and wailed. "Waaa! Waaa!"

Grandpa stepped up to Rachel and frowned. "You shouldn't have yelled at the boy like that. He didn't bump your arm on purpose. It was an accident."

The man nodded and looked at Rachel. "As you well know, accidents do happen." He reached into his pocket and pulled out a lollipop, which he handed to Gerald.

Gerald quit crying, took a seat in one corner of the room, and stuck the lollipop in his mouth.

"If you'll come with me," Grandpa said to the man, "we'll find just the right plant for your wife. I was planning to put some plants on sale for 50 percent off next week, but if you'd like one now, I'll give it to you for the sale price since the one you really wanted is ruined."

"Thank you. I appreciate that," the man said.

The man must think it's my fault, because he didn't offer me a lollipop, Rachel thought as she cleaned up the dirt that had spilled on the floor. *I wish Gerald hadn't come to stay with us. He's nothing but trouble!*

A short time later, the man stepped up to Rachel and handed her a dollar.

"What's this for?" she asked.

"I had only one lollipop, or I would have given you one, too." He patted Rachel's shoulder. "Your grandfather's lucky to have you working here. I can see that you're a real good worker."

Rachel smiled up at him. It felt nice to be appreciated.

As Rachel and Gerald walked up to the house, Rachel

thought about the dollar the man had given her. *Should I put it in my piggy bank and save it toward something I really want, or should I buy some candy the next time we go to town? I think I'll save it for now,* she finally decided.

"Should I set the table for lunch?" Rachel asked Mom when she and Gerald stepped into the kitchen.

Mom tapped her foot. Her eyebrows scrunched together above her thin nose as she frowned. "You forgot to make your bed this morning, Rachel."

"I was planning to make it after Mary left, but when Grandpa asked me to help in the greenhouse, I forgot all about making my bed," Rachel explained.

Mom tapped her foot a couple more times. "No excuses, Rachel. I want you to go upstairs and make it right now. When you're done, you can set the table for lunch."

"Okay." Rachel trudged up the stairs. *Thump. Thump. Thump.* She was almost at the top when she heard another set of footsteps, a little softer than hers. *Thump. Thump. Thump.*

She turned and saw Gerald behind her. "Oh, great!" She was beginning to think the little boy had become her shadow.

"I'm busy, Gerald. Go back downstairs!" Rachel rushed into her room and slammed the door. Her stomach rumbled, so she hurried to make the bed.

Tap! Tap! Tap!

"Who is it?" Rachel called.

Tap! Tap! Tap!

Rachel groaned and opened the door.

"Whatcha doin'?" Gerald asked as he darted into the room.

Rachel pointed to the bed. "I just finished making my bed."

Gerald shook his head. "God made the bed!"

"No, *I* made my bed."

Gerald folded his arms and stared at Rachel as if she were stupid. "God made everything!"

Rachel thought about what she'd told Gerald the night before, when they'd been looking at the moon in the sky. "That's right, Gerald. God made everything. He made the trees that were turned into wood to make my bed."

Gerald pointed to Rachel and shook his head. "Rachel didn't make the bed."

Rachel sighed. How could she make Gerald understand what she'd meant about making her bed?

Suddenly, an idea popped into her head. She pulled back the covers, messed up the bed, and made it all over again. "*I* made the bed," she said with a nod.

Gerald shook his head. "God made the bed."

Rachel pulled the covers back and made the bed again. This time she said, "I pulled the covers over my bed."

Gerald nodded and said, "God made the bed! Rachel covered the bed."

Rachel smiled and took Gerald's hand. "Now that we've got that settled, let's go downstairs and have some lunch."

Chapter 11

The Worst Possible News

Wearing a backpack over her shoulders and carrying her lunch pail in one hand and a jump rope in the other hand, Rachel hurried up the path leading to the schoolhouse.

"Slow down!" Jacob hollered. "You can't be that anxious to get to school!"

Rachel turned to face him. "Today's the first day of school, and I don't want to be late. Besides, going to school is better than dealing with Gerald at home." She sighed. "I'll be glad when his folks get back and he goes home where he belongs."

Jacob shook his finger at Rachel the way Mom sometimes did. "You shouldn't talk about Gerald like that. He's our cousin, and he's a nice little boy."

"That's easy for you to say." Rachel wrinkled her nose. "Ever since Gerald came to stay with us, all he's done is hang around me and ask a bunch of silly questions."

Jacob shrugged. "I guess that means he likes you more than anyone else in the family."

"I doubt it." Rachel started walking fast again.

"Slow down!"

"I want to get to school early so I can use the new jump rope I bought the other day."

Jacob grunted as he caught up to her. "That was a dumm thing to buy with the money you saved."

"It was not a dumm thing to buy!" Rachel raced ahead of Jacob. He thought everything she did was dumb!

When Rachel entered the school yard, she set her backpack and lunch pail on the ground near a tree. Then she found a level spot on the grass, opened her jump rope, and started to jump. *One. . .two. . .three. . .* She never missed a beat. *Four. . .five. . .six. . .* Her arms swung up and over in perfect rhythm with her feet.

"Did you know. . .what Rachel did. . .the other day. . . ?"

Rachel's ears perked up when she heard her name mentioned. She glanced to the left. Audra stood beside Orlie, whispering something in his ear.

Rachel gripped the handles of the jump rope a little tighter. *I wonder what Audra said to Orlie about me.*

Seven. . .eight. . . She'd better not have said anything bad about me. Nine. . .ten. . . Maybe I should go over there and ask.

Ding! Ding! Ding! The school bell rang, calling everyone inside. Rachel stopped jumping. She'd have to wait until later to learn what Audra had said to Orlie.

Racing across the school yard, the scholars burst into the schoolhouse.

"My, my," exclaimed Teacher Elizabeth as Rachel stepped inside, "it looks like everyone's happy to be back in school!"

Rachel forced a smile. She had been happy until she'd heard Audra whispering something to Orlie about her.

She put her lunch pail and jump rope on the shelf over on the girls' side of the coatroom; then she shuffled to her seat. After she sat down, she glanced across the aisle where Audra sat.

Audra looked at Rachel and smiled. "It's good to be back in school, isn't it?"

Rachel shrugged her shoulders then turned her attention to the front of the room when Elizabeth rang the little bell on her desk. "Good morning, boys and girls."

"Good morning," the scholars all said.

Everyone stood to recite the Lord's Prayer and sing songs.

Then Elizabeth went to the blackboard. She'd just put the arithmetic assignment on the board when Rachel heard a familiar *bzzz. . .bzzz. . .bzzz. . .*

She looked up and saw a bee buzz in front of her face. She ducked. It zipped across the aisle and circled Audra's head.

Audra squealed, jumped out of her seat, and raced to

the back of the room.

Audra's reaction came as no surprise to Rachel, for she knew Audra was afraid of bugs. And after Rachel's encounter with the bee that had stung her nose, she was a little nervous about a bee buzzing around her, too.

The bee continued to buzz and circle everyone in the room. Soon all the girls, including Rachel, joined Audra at the back of the room.

The boys jumped out of their seats and chased after the bee.

"I'll get that pesky iem!" Orlie shouted.

"Children, children, please take your seats." Elizabeth clapped her hands. "It's just a little bee; there's no need to panic." She looked at Jacob and said, "Would you please open the window? Maybe the bee will fly out."

Jacob hurried to do as Elizabeth had asked, but the bee kept buzzing and didn't go anywhere near the window.

Jacob grabbed his notebook and swatted at the bee. *Whoosh*!

The bee stopped buzzing and dropped to the floor.

"Is it dead?" Orlie called.

Jacob shook his head. "Its wings are still moving, so I think it's just stunned." He tore a piece of paper from his notebook, bent down, and scooped up the bee. Then he marched across the room and tossed it out the window.

Sighs of relief sounded around the room as Jacob shut the window.

"You may all take your seats now," Elizabeth said to the scholars.

Rachel followed behind Audra. She wished there was time to ask her what she'd said to Orlie when they were outside before school started. But she knew that would have to wait until recess.

When recess finally came, Rachel hurried out the door, tripped on the porch step, and—*floop!*—went down on her knees!

"Always trouble somewhere," she mumbled as she picked herself up.

"Are you okay?" Teacher Elizabeth asked, rushing to Rachel.

"I—I think so." Tears stung the backs of Rachel's eyes as she struggled not to cry. Her knee hurt, but she didn't want anyone to think she was acting like a baby.

"Let's go inside so I can look at your knees," Elizabeth said. "They might be bleeding."

Rachel nodded and limped into the schoolhouse. After she'd taken a seat at her desk, she lifted one corner of her dress. Sure enough, both knees had been scraped and were bleeding.

"I'll get some bandages and antiseptic." Elizabeth quickly went to her desk and opened a drawer. She returned with two bandages and a bottle of antiseptic, which she put over the scrapes on Rachel's knees. "There now, that should feel better," she said after she'd put the bandages in place.

"Danki." Rachel winced as she stood.

"If your knees hurt, maybe you should stay inside for recess today."

Rachel shook her head. If she stayed inside, she wouldn't get to talk to Audra. "I'm okay. My knees don't hurt real bad."

Elizabeth patted Rachel's shoulder. "Okay. Just be careful not to fall again."

"I'll be careful."

When Rachel stepped outside, she spotted Audra on one of the swings. Phoebe Byler sat on the other swing.

Rachel frowned. At this rate, she'd never get to talk to Audra!

Maybe I should talk to Orlie instead, Rachel thought. *I can ask him what Audra said.*

She limped her way over to the fence, where Orlie sat with Jacob and Brian.

"What do you want?" Brian asked, glaring at Rachel. She wondered if he was afraid she might say something about his bed-wetting problem.

"I need to talk to Orlie for a minute."

"About what?" Orlie asked.

"I just want to know—"

"Go play with the girls and quit bothering us," Brian said.

Rachel clenched her fingers, tempted to nibble on the end of a fingernail.

"You heard what Brian said." Jacob flapped his hand at Rachel. "Go away now—shoo, little bensel!"

Rachel flapped her hand right back at him. "I'm not a silly child!"

"Jah, you are."

"No, I'm not. You're a silly child!"

Before Jacob could respond, Rachel raced over to the swings. "Can you stop swinging now?" she called to Audra.

"How come?"

"I need to talk to you."

"About what?"

"If you'll get off the swing and come over here, I'll tell you."

Audra shook her head. "I'm having too much fun. You can talk to me from where I am."

"What were you telling Orlie about me before school started?" Rachel shouted.

Whoosh! Audra's swing went so high that the ties on her kapp blew out behind her. "What was that?"

"What were you telling Orlie about me before school started?"

"I wasn't telling him anything about you!"

"Jah, you were. I heard you mention my name."

Audra halted her swing, tipped her head, and looked

at Rachel as if she'd lost her mind. "I don't know what you're talking about."

"I heard you say, 'Did you know what Rachel did the other day?'"

Audra shook her head. "I never said that."

"Jah, you did."

"No, I didn't. What I said was, 'Did you know that Rachel's cousin lives on a dairy farm?'"

"But you said something about what Rachel did the other day," Rachel insisted. "What were you telling Orlie that I did the other day?"

"You're jumping to conclusions," Audra said. "I wasn't talking about you at all. After I mentioned that your cousin lives on a dairy farm, I said that the other day my daed decided to buy some goats because he likes goat's milk better than cow's milk."

"So you weren't saying anything bad about me to Orlie?"

"Of course not. You're my good friend. I'd never talk bad about you."

Rachel sighed with relief. "You're my good friend, too, Audra."

When Rachel and Jacob arrived home from school that afternoon, Mom had a snack waiting for them on the kitchen table. Beside two glasses of chocolate milk was a plate of chocolate cupcakes. Mom placed one glass in front of Rachel and one in front of Jacob; then she gave each of them a cupcake. "I'm going upstairs to check on Gerald," she said. "He should be awake from his nap by now."

When Mom left the room, Rachel studied the snacks on the table.

"Your glass of milk's fuller than mine, and your cupcake's bigger, too," she said, frowning at Jacob. "I think Mom favors you over me."

"Don't be lecherich, Rachel. Mom doesn't favor any of her kinner. She loves us all the same."

"I'm not being ridiculous." Rachel took a drink of milk and wiped her lips with a napkin. "Since you got the most chocolate milk, I think you should give me the bigger cupcake."

"No way! Mom gave me this cupcake, and I'm eating it right now!" Jacob quickly peeled back the paper and popped the whole cupcake into his mouth. "Umm. . .this is sure good!"

Rachel wrinkled her nose. "That's disgusting, Jacob! Don't you know you're not supposed to talk with your mouth full?"

"I can do whatever I want; you're not my boss." Jacob grabbed his glass of milk and took a big drink. Some of the milk ran out of his mouth and trickled down his chin.

Rachel looked away. She wished Mom would have come back into the room and seen Jacob acting so rude. He'd be in big trouble, and if Mom had been favoring

Jacob by giving him the fullest glass of milk and the biggest cupcake, she'd probably never do it again.

"Well, guess I'd better get out to the fields and see about helping Pap and Henry," Jacob said, pushing his chair away from the table.

"That won't be necessary," Mom said as she and a sleepy-eyed Gerald entered the kitchen.

"Why not?" Jacob asked, wiping his mouth with his hand.

"Your daed and Henry went to town to run some errands." Mom motioned to the plate of cupcakes. "So if you'd like to have more to eat, go right ahead."

"Since I don't have to work this afternoon, I think I'll go fishing in the creek." Jacob grabbed a cupcake. "I'll take this along!"

"Can I go fishing, too?" Rachel called as Jacob headed for the door.

"Suit yourself!" Jacob opened the door and rushed outside.

Rachel jumped up and followed. She'd just stepped onto the porch when she spotted Aunt Karen's buggy pulling into the yard. "Aunt Karen's here," she called to Mom over her shoulder. "She must have come to get Gerald."

Mom joined Rachel on the porch. "Would you mind keeping an eye on Gerald while Aunt Karen and I visit awhile?" she asked.

Rachel groaned. "Do I have to, Mom? I wanted to go fishing with Jacob."

"You can join him later—after Aunt Karen and Gerald go home."

Rachel sighed. "Okay, Mom. I'll take Gerald to the living room and read a story to him."

"I'd rather you get him a cupcake and go outside," Mom said. "Hannah's taking a nap in the living room."

"Oh, all right," Rachel said. "I'll take Gerald outside on the porch, and we can blow some bubbles after he's had his snack."

A short time later, Rachel and Gerald were seated on the back porch steps, blowing bubbles.

"Blos!" Gerald shouted as he raced into the yard and chased the bubbles Rachel had made.

Rachel laughed and made several more bubbles. She waved them in the air so they floated into the yard.

"I'm glad you told me this. It's important that we pray for him."

Rachel heard Aunt Karen talking through the open kitchen window, and her ears perked up. She became especially interested when she heard Mom mention Jacob's name.

"Blow more blos!" Gerald hollered as he jumped up and down.

"Okay, okay." Rachel blew several more bubbles, and

Gerald chased after them, giggling and leaping into the air like a wild goat.

"I feel so bad that Jacob's sick and might not make it," Aunt Karen said through the open window.

Rachel gasped. *Jacob's sick and might not make it?*

Might not make what? Rachel wondered. Then she realized that's what people said sometimes when someone was dying—that they may not make it!

No, no, it just couldn't be! Even though she and Jacob had their share of misunderstandings, and even though he teased her, Rachel didn't want him to die.

"It's always hard when we have to say good-bye to a loved one." Mom's voice sounded very sad, and Rachel wondered if she'd been crying. She couldn't blame her if she had. Hearing that Jacob was sick and would probably die made Rachel feel like crying, too.

No wonder Mom gave Jacob the biggest cupcake and fullest glass of milk, Rachel thought. *Mom wanted to be sure that Jacob's happy.*

Rachel's hands shook so badly she dropped the bubble wand. *I've got to do something to make Jacob's last days as happy as they can be. Even though Jacob teases me a lot and makes me mad sometimes, he needs to know how much I love him.*

Rachel rested her elbows on her knees and closed her eyes. She couldn't tell anyone what she'd heard. If she did, she'd be in trouble for eavesdropping again. And if she told anyone that Jacob was sick and might not make it, that would be gossiping.

Dear God, Rachel silently prayed, *please show me what I can do for Jacob.*

That night after supper, Mom asked Jacob and Rachel to do the dishes while she fed and diapered the baby.

"Jacob doesn't have to help," Rachel was quick to say. "I can do the dishes by myself."

Mom's forehead wrinkled as she stared at Rachel over the top of her glasses. "Are you sure?"

Rachel nodded. "I'm very sure. Jacob's free to do whatever he pleases."

Jacob grinned and thumped Rachel's back. "Danki, little sister."

At least he hadn't called her a little bensel this time. Even if he had, Rachel wouldn't have said anything about it. From now on, she was determined to be nice to Jacob.

"Have you fed Buddy yet?" she asked when Jacob started to leave the room.

"Not yet. I'm going out to do that right now," he called over his shoulder.

"I'll do it," Rachel offered. "Why don't you find a comfortable chair and rest?"

Jacob turned to face her. "If you're expecting me to pay you for feeding Buddy, you can forget it."

She shook her head. "I don't want any money."

"Do you want me to do one of your chores in exchange for feeding my hund?"

She shook her head.

Jacob's eyes narrowed into tiny slits. "What's up, Rachel? You hate feeding Buddy. You always complain because he jumps up and licks your face."

Rachel blushed. There was no way she could tell Jacob that she knew he was sick. If Mom hadn't told Aunt Karen about it, Rachel wouldn't have known the truth, either. She felt sure that Mom hadn't told Jacob he was dying. If he knew, he wouldn't be acting so cheerful.

Rachel touched Jacob's arm. "I—I just want to help you, because I—" She swallowed around the lump in her throat, hoping she wouldn't cry. "Be–because I love you."

Jacob stared at Rachel for a long time. Then his face broke into a wide smile. "If you really want to feed Buddy, then it's fine with me. I'll go to my room and read a book." He patted Rachel on the shoulder a couple of times. "I love you, too, little bensel."

Chapter 12

A Big Surprise

"I'm thirsty. Would you get me a glass of water?" Jacob asked Rachel when he entered the kitchen the following morning.

Normally, Rachel would have said, "Get it yourself." However, since Jacob was on the brink of death, she figured she should do what he asked. Rachel smiled and said, "Jah, sure, Jacob. I'd be happy to get you a glass of water."

"Danki." Jacob pulled out a chair at the table and sat down. "I sure feel tired this morning. Wish I didn't have to go to school," he said with a yawn.

"Actually, you won't be going to school this morning," Mom said. "You have an appointment with Dr. Adams, remember?"

Jacob stretched his arms over his head and yawned again. "Oh, that's right; I forgot."

"If you're not feeling well enough to go to school after your appointment, you'll come home with me," Mom said.

Jacob nodded. "By then, I'll probably be more tired than I already am."

Rachel's heart went out to Jacob. She couldn't imagine what he must be going through or how bad he felt.

"Waaa! Waaa!"

"It sounds like your little sister is awake and needs to be fed." Mom patted Rachel's shoulder. "Since Jacob won't be walking to school with you this morning, I'll ask Grandpa to hitch his buggy and take you there." She hurried from the room before Rachel could respond.

I wish Mom would stop treating me like a boppli, Rachel thought. *She let me walk to school by myself a couple of times, so why not today?*

She hung her head. *I guess I shouldn't be thinking such thoughts. Mom's worried about Jacob. She's probably worried about me, too.*

"Where's my glass of water?" Jacob asked impatiently. "I'm really thirsty."

Rachel hurried to the sink and filled a glass with cold water. When she handed it to Jacob, she noticed how tired he looked. Maybe he was doing too much and needed to rest more. Maybe when Jacob saw the doctor today, he'd be told to take it easy. And maybe, if Rachel kept doing all of Jacob's chores, he would live a little longer.

As Rachel traveled to school in Grandpa's buggy, all she could think about was Jacob. She couldn't imagine how things would be without him. She'd have to go to school every day by herself. She would miss playing in the creek with Jacob on hot summer days. She would miss jumping on the trampoline with him, too. She might even miss Jacob's teasing and calling her "little bensel."

Rachel swallowed hard, trying to push down the lump she felt in her throat. She wouldn't be the only one who'd miss Jacob if he died. Mom, Dad, Henry, Esther, Rudy, Grandpa Schrock, Grandpa and Grandma Yoder, Jacob's friends at school—even Buddy would miss Jacob. How sad that baby Hannah would grow up never knowing her brother Jacob.

Clip-clop. Clip-clop. The horse whinnied and plodded slowly up the road.

Grandpa clicked his tongue and shook the reins. "Get up there, boy! If you don't get moving, you'll make Rachel late for school!"

"I won't be late. Riding in the buggy is much faster than walking." Rachel glanced over at Grandpa. Did he know about Jacob's condition? Should she say something about what she'd heard Mom say to Aunt Karen the other day? Maybe it would be best to keep quiet. If she said anything to Grandpa, he might accuse her of eavesdropping and gossiping.

Maybe I should mention Jacob's name, Rachel thought. *If Grandpa already knows that Jacob is sick, he might say something about it to me.*

Rachel leaned closer to Grandpa and said, "Have you noticed anything different about Jacob lately?"

"Nothing special." Grandpa shrugged. "Although he does seem to have grown a few inches over the summer."

"Uh-huh." Rachel sat quietly for several minutes. She decided to ask another question. "Does it seem to you like he doesn't have much energy these days?"

Grandpa gave the reins another good shake. "You mean my lazy *gaul* [horse]?"

"No, I mean Jacob."

"Can't really say for sure. Guess you'd have to ask your daed that question, since Jacob worked in the fields with him and Henry all summer." Grandpa tugged his beard. "Jah, your daed's the one to ask about Jacob all right."

Rachel leaned back in her seat and closed her eyes. *This conversation is getting me nowhere. Either Grandpa doesn't know anything about Jacob being sick, or he doesn't want to talk about it. I need to talk to someone about this, but who can I trust not to say anything?*

"Whoa!" The buggy lurched, and Rachel's eyes snapped open.

"I hate to wake you from your nap, but we're here," Grandpa said with a wide grin.

"I wasn't sleeping, Grandpa. I was thinking."

He chuckled and patted Rachel's arm. "You're a daydreamer, same as your mamm used to be when she was a maedel."

Rachel couldn't argue with that. She did like to daydream. It was fun to imagine herself going places and doing things she hadn't done before.

She reached down and grabbed her backpack and lunch pail from the floor of the buggy. "Danki for the ride. See you after school, Grandpa."

He nodded and smiled. "If your mamm and Jacob don't get home from Jacob's appointment before school lets out, I'll be back to pick you up this afternoon."

"Okay." Rachel hopped out of the buggy. *If Grandpa knows Jacob went to see the doctor today, then he must know that Jacob is sick,* she thought. *I think maybe he doesn't want to talk about it because he doesn't want me to know. Everyone else in the family probably knows. They haven't told me because they think I'm too young to understand. I'd hoped after Hannah was born that they'd realize I'm growing up, but, no, they think I'm still a boppli.*

As Rachel headed for the school yard, she spotted Audra standing by the swings. *Maybe I should talk to her about Jacob,* she decided. *I can't keep the horrible news I've learned about him to myself any longer.*

Rachel dashed over to Audra. "I—I need to talk to you," she said, clasping Audra's arm.

"What's wrong?" Audra asked. "You look *umgerennt* [upset]."

"I am upset." Tears welled in Rachel's eyes. "Jacob's sick and might not make it. He's not here today because

Mom took him to see the doctor."

Audra's eyes widened, and her mouth formed an O. "Ach, that's baremlich!"

"I know it's terrible." Rachel sniffed and swiped at the tears trickling down her cheeks. "Sometimes I get upset with Jacob when he teases me, but I still love him. I—I don't want my bruder to die."

"No, of course you don't." Audra gave Rachel a hug. "I wouldn't want my bruder to die, either."

"Please promise you won't—"

Ding! Ding! Ding!

"There's the school bell. We'd better get inside." Audra gave Rachel's arm a pat and hurried away before Rachel could finish her sentence.

I hope Audra doesn't tell anyone what I told her about Jacob, Rachel thought as she blew her nose and trudged up the schoolhouse stairs.

"Good morning boys and girls," Elizabeth said after the scholars had taken seats behind their desks.

"Good morning, Elizabeth," everyone said.

Audra's hand went up.

"What is it, Audra?" Elizabeth asked.

"Jacob Yoder's not here this morning because he went to see the doctor." Audra looked over at Rachel and said, "Tell Elizabeth what you told me about Jacob."

Rachel's heart pounded as she shook her head. She

hoped Audra wouldn't repeat what she'd said.

"What's this all about?" Elizabeth asked, moving closer to Audra's desk.

"Jacob's sick and might not make it," Audra blurted.

Elizabeth's forehead wrinkled, and she looked over at Rachel. "Is that true?"

Rachel nodded slowly as a lump formed in her throat. Now the whole class knew. They were all looking at her with sympathy on their faces.

"I had no idea Jacob was sick," Elizabeth said. "What's wrong with him, Rachel?"

Rachel shrugged. "I–I'm not sure. I just know that he's sick and might not make it."

"I'm real sorry to hear this." Elizabeth's eyes looked watery. Rachel wondered if her teacher might break down and cry in front of the whole class. Rachel hoped not, because if Elizabeth started to cry, then she'd end up crying, too.

Elizabeth moved over to Rachel's desk. "As soon as we're done with the morning songs and have said the Lord's Prayer, I'll have everyone in class make Jacob a get-well card."

A get-well card? Oh, no, Rachel thought. *Now Mom will know I was listening to her conversation with Aunt Karen.*

When Rachel arrived home from school that day, her

stomach felt as if it were tied in knots. Jacob hadn't come to school at all today, which made her think he'd probably gotten sicker. To make matters worse, Teacher Elizabeth was planning to come over this afternoon with the get-well cards the scholars had made. Once that happened, Mom would guess that Rachel was the one who'd told. Then Rachel would be in trouble for eavesdropping and gossiping.

"You can go up to the house to change your clothes and have a snack while I unhitch the horse and get him put away," Grandpa said. "Then after you get your homework done, I could use your help in the greenhouse."

Rachel nodded. Maybe she'd be working in the greenhouse when Elizabeth came over with the get-well cards. That would keep her out of trouble with Mom for a little while.

Rachel hurried into the house and slipped quietly upstairs to her room. When she'd changed out of her school dress, she took her homework out of her backpack and flopped onto the bed.

She'd just opened her spelling book when she heard, *Tap! Tap! Tap!*

"Rachel, are you in there?" Mom called through the closed door.

"Jah, Mom. I'm getting ready to do my homework."

"Come down to the kitchen to do it," Mom said. "I've got some fresh fruit cups and milk waiting for you."

"Okay, I'm coming." Rachel stayed on the bed a few minutes longer, thinking things over; then she finally gathered up her spelling book and left the room.

Downstairs, she found Mom and Jacob sitting at the kitchen table. Mom had a cup of tea, and Jacob had a glass of milk. The left side of Jacob's face looked kind of puffy. His eyelids looked heavy, too, and his shoulders were slumped. He didn't look well at all!

Rachel touched Jacob's shoulder. "I—uh—want you to know something."

"What's that?" he asked.

"I'm sorry for anything I've ever said or done to upset you."

Jacob leaned back in his chair and looked at Rachel with an odd expression. It made her want to cry and beg him not to die. "What's wrong with you, Rachel?" he asked, tapping her arm. "Are you *grank* [sick]?"

"No, of course not. I'm just real sorry that you—"

"Oh, look," Mom said as she peered out the kitchen window, "your schoolteacher's here." She looked at Rachel and frowned. "You didn't do anything wrong at school today, did you?"

Rachel gulped. She had done something wrong. She'd blabbed to Audra about Jacob being sick, and then Audra had told their teacher. Now Elizabeth was here, probably with the get-well cards the scholars had made for Jacob.

Rachel figured she'd better explain things before Elizabeth came inside, but before she could open her mouth, Mom rushed out the door.

"I need to tell you something," Rachel said as she stepped onto the porch behind Mom.

"Later, Rachel. I need to see what your teacher wants." Mom hurried down the steps and out to Elizabeth's buggy.

Rachel quickly followed.

"Hello, Rachel," Elizabeth said as she stepped out of the buggy. "Did you tell your mamm that I'd be coming by this afternoon?"

"Uh, no. Not yet," Rachel stammered.

Mom looked down at Rachel. "You knew Elizabeth was coming by and you never mentioned it?"

Rachel's face grew hot. "Well, I—"

"I brought some cards that the scholars made for Jacob." Elizabeth reached into her buggy and pulled out a paper sack. "If he's feeling up to company I'd like to come inside and give them to him."

Mom gave Elizabeth a peculiar look over the top of her glasses, but then she shrugged and said, "Jah, sure. You're welcome to come inside."

Elizabeth handed the sack of cards to Rachel, and then she tied her horse to the hitching rail.

Rachel wished she could take the sack out to the fire pit and burn it, but she knew she'd be in trouble for that.

There was no getting around it: Mom was about to find out that Rachel had been eavesdropping and gossiping again. That didn't bother her nearly as much as knowing that Jacob's health was getting worse every day, and that he might not be with them much longer.

With a heavy heart, Rachel followed Mom and Elizabeth into the house. When they entered the kitchen, Elizabeth placed the paper sack on the table in front of Jacob, put one hand on his shoulder, and said, "I have a surprise for you, Jacob. The scholars made you these get-well cards." Tears welled in her eyes. "We're all very sorry to hear how sick you are."

Jacob's eyebrows shot up. "Huh?"

"Rachel told us about it. She said you weren't in school today because you'd gone to the doctor's."

Jacob opened the sack and pulled out one of the cards. There was a picture of a big, shaggy red dog on the front. The inside of the card read:

> *I'm sorry to hear that you're sick and might not make it. Buddy will miss you when you're gone, and so will I.*
> *Your friend, Orlie Troyer.*

Jacob scratched the side of his head and gave Mom a questioning look. "Am I sick and don't know it?"

Mom shook her head. "Ach no, Jacob! I don't know

why the scholars think you're sick, unless—" She looked over at Rachel and frowned. "Did you make up some story about Jacob being gone from school today because he's sick?"

Rachel shifted from one leg to the other. "I—uh— didn't make up the story. I—I was just repeating what'd I heard you say to Aunt Karen the other day."

Deep wrinkles formed in Mom's forehead as she rubbed the bridge of her nose. "What exactly did you hear me say to her?"

"You said Jacob was very sick and that he might not make it."

"That's what Rachel told me at school today," Elizabeth said.

Mom gasped.

Jacob groaned and dropped his head to the table.

"Karen and I weren't talking about *our* Jacob," Mom said. "We were talking about my cousin, whose name is also Jacob. Cousin Jacob lives in Kentucky, and he's very sick." She pushed her glasses onto the bridge of her nose and squinted at Rachel. "For your information, Jacob went to see the dentist today, not the doctor."

Jacob lifted his head from the table.

Rachel covered her mouth with her hand. She was sorry to hear about Mom's cousin but relieved to know that Jacob wasn't sick.

Mom shook her finger at Rachel. "See the trouble

you've caused by eavesdropping and then running off to school and gossiping about what you *thought* you'd heard? That's how misunderstandings get started, you know."

Rachel stared at the floor as she slowly nodded. "I–I'm sorry. It was just a big mistake."

"You should have asked me about what you'd heard instead of jumping to conclusions," Mom said.

Tears coursed down Rachel's cheeks. "I know that, and I promise I'll never do it again."

Rachel leaned over and hugged Jacob. "I'm glad you're not sick." *Sniff! Sniff!* "I hope you'll stick around for a very long time."

He nodded and grinned. "I've gotta stick around, or else who would be here to tease you, little bensel?"

Rachel poked Jacob's arm. "I'm happy you're sticking around, but if you're going to keep teasing me, then I think you should know that I'll tease you right back."

Jacob took a drink of milk and wiped his mouth with the back of his hand. "That's not such a big surprise, but I can deal with it."

Rachel took a seat at the table and pushed the paper sack closer to Jacob. "You may as well look at the rest of your get-well cards, don't you think?"

Jacob nodded and rubbed the side of his face. "I may not be sick, but my mouth's kind of sore from being open so long at the dentist's. Maybe the get-well cards will make me feel better."

Mom handed Rachel a glass of milk, and Rachel took a big drink. From now on she would never intentionally listen in on anyone's conversation. If she accidentally heard someone say something she didn't understand, she would ask questions, not jump to conclusions!

Recipe for Rachel's
Homemade Bubble Solution

¼ cup liquid dishwashing detergent
¾ cup cold water
5 drops of glycerin (available at most pharmacies)
A few drops of food coloring (if you want colorful
  bubbles)

Measure out the detergent, water, and glycerin into a
container with a cover and stir gently. Note: The longer
you let the mixture set, the larger the bubbles will be and
the longer they seem to last.

Other books by Wanda E. Brunstetter

Children's Fiction

RACHEL YODER—ALWAYS TROUBLE SOMEWHERE SERIES

School's Out!
Back to School
Out of Control
New Beginnings
A Happy Heart
Just Plain Foolishness
Jumping to Conclusions
Growing Up

The Wisdom of Solomon

Adult Fiction

INDIANA COUSINS SERIES
SISTERS OF HOLMES COUNTY SERIES
BRIDES OF WEBSTER COUNTY SERIES
DAUGHTERS OF LANCASTER COUNTY SERIES
BRIDES OF LANCASTER COUNTY SERIES

White Christmas Pie

Nonfiction

Wanda E. Brunstetter's Amish Friends Cookbook
Wanda E. Brunstetter's Amish Friends Cookbook Volume 2
The Simple Life

Also available from Barbour Publishing